# The Fourth Door

Maria Tenace

*This book is a work of fantasy.
Characters and situations are the result of the
author's imagination and have the only purpose of
giving truth to the story.
Any similarity or reference to events, places or people,
living or dead, is purely coincidental.
Each reference to the Cuban people and folklore,
especially of Yoruba origins, wants to be a tribute to
this extraordinary land, rich in historical, cultural
and religious references, present and past.*

English translation
Fatima Immacolata Pretta

Dedicated to…


This novel is dedicated to brave people who despite the dark manage to grasp all the nuances of life.
And to all those who want to continue to be the bright shade in someone's dark life, despite everything.


To my father who never told me how to live, but he lived and made me observe how he did it.
With an open mind.

# Table of Contents

# PROLOGUE

- I think I've been here before.

The girl, walking along the corridor, touched the white wall and followed the path with two fingers of her right hand.

She remembered the feeling of the cold floor, the feeling of his bare feet coming off and rising slowly, alternating in steps.

She also felt the long white nightgown, lightly brushing her ankles, as well as the light weight of the dark braids that fell on her shoulders, just as she wore them as a child.

She sensed the presence of a person by her side, but could not understand who it was.

All that white bothered her a lot.

The reverberation of the cold light of the neon lights attached to the ceiling did not allow her to have a clear vision but she continued, dazzled and confused, with her gaze fixed on her.

- Have you ever had recurring and detailed dreams, so realistic that you cannot understand if you are sleeping or are awake? - Asked the girl.

- I think you shouldn't make confusion between dream and life.

The calm and reassuring voice answered. Then she continued:

- I will ask you another question and I know you will forgive me: have you ever been on a train and from the window see the one next to it move? The girl nodded with a nod.

- Well see, we've all had at least once, the distorted perception that our train is leaving. Instead it stands there, motionless.
We are still and also our train.
It is a bit like life, we believe it is something personal in constant movement and evolution, but only when the empty tracks are revealed, beyond the glass, do we end up realizing that we are still stuck in the same place.
In the same way, only when we perceive the emptiness that we have in the soul, can we realize how deeply we are bogged down in our pools, made of fears and regrets, disappointments, anger and all the ballast of negative feelings that we carry with us.
We take for ourselves some episodes stolen from the life of others, we put them together with crumbled parts of ours and we have the illusion of an authentic experience.
But that's not our life.
It is the life that we would like but that we do not have, and it is this lack that creates that emptiness.
Perhaps there is not even a remedy for that black hole in the soul and the human being, too greedy and curious about everything, should not waste precious time looking for it.
-What do you mean? I don't understand ...
The girl stopped to think.

- I mean, basically, if every person, man or woman, looked inside, deep inside, who would ever admit to being completely satisfied or happy, one hundred per cent, of the life they lead?

A car, a job, a family, a full fridge, a new sofa, a dog or a cat.

It doesn't matter if you have all this, all you need and even the superfluous. Man will always feel that something is missing, there will always be a hole, large or small that he will not know how to fill. For some it is the evil of existing, others will call it psychic pain, others with still different names. The time has come for you to understand how to fill that void. Try Stella, maybe it's the right time.

At the end of the corridor, in front of the fourth door, the presence handed her a small golden key which she grasped with some hesitation.

- Open and look who or what is inside, just like you did with the other three doors before.

So, as if she were projected onto a screen, she found herself living someone else's life.

# 1

## *MARTA*

Looking at her figure reflected in the large mirror in her room, standing in front of her, Martha asked her: what do you want, what are you missing?

But she already knew that she would only move her lips and eyes in sync.

She stopped looking, she understood that all she needed to pass the time was a new canvas, a brush, tempera paints and Valium's bottle of her mother.

That bottle, that modern elixir that allowed her to appear so perfect and socially "acceptable", so much so that she too was a drug addict.

And this was the ritual of the evening, before the shadows entered their room.

She looked out the window and thought it hadn't been long.

She would have liked to feel the metallic smell of the rain that, at that moment, was drawing fractures on the glass that seemed to be sending it to pieces, at any moment.

Many asked her why she painted only still lifes.

People were convinced that it was desperation, death or other shit like that, but she didn't have the answer and didn't pretend to have it, no more.

She only knew that she liked to paint woven baskets of rattan, with dried fruit and autumn leaves inside, using the shades of colors that most relaxed her, especially the brown, warm, orange ones.

The sliding of the brush on the canvas, after imbibing it in the color, gave it a serenity difficult to explain. It was the most similar to the ecstasy there is, perhaps it was precisely that creative ecstasy that all painters have experienced at least once in their lives and that only in the older ones, originating from inner motions, in the end generated masterpieces.

She spread the colors on the figures at regular intervals, creating a rhythm, an alternation of full and empty spaces and the empty surface became a score.

Time was dictated by the moment: it could be the chirping of a cicada as the tinkling of wind chimes on the window opened in summer.

In that instant, the sound of the rain on the glass acted as a metronome, a fortuitous sequence of beats that followed one another and gave life to the sound. She heard thunder and this made her think of her grandmother who smelled of a good and clean old woman, thanks to her jasmine colony.

She always told her a story, when in the bed she jumped at the sound of thunder, looking for the cold and flourishing hands that held hers to give her courage.

"It all started with Saint Peter's mother, a stingy and flawed woman. Passed to a better life, the woman was relegated to hell to pay for her sins. One day Peter, grieved for her, asked Jesus to bring her up to Heaven.

Jesus replied that the woman had made too many mistakes in life, but if he had found even one good deed, for love of Peter, he would have made her go up.

The saint then consulted his mother's book of life and discovered only one good deed: she had given to a poor man the skins of the potatoes she was peeling.

With those peelings the angels made a rope that was lowered into hell.

The rope was very fragile, but sufficient for the light transport of a single soul.

The woman, happy, grabbed it immediately, but at that point other souls of the damned surrounded her to climb up behind her.

The woman screamed, warning the others to stay back.

The rope was just for her and she started kicking to keep the damned away.

But in doing so, the fragile rope broke.

The cries of anger, together with the thud of the woman who had fallen back into hell, became the sound of thunder that often accompanies thunderstorms. So you have nothing to fear, it's her own fault."

How much she wished she was with her at the time. She decided the next day she would have called Alessandra, her best friend.

- I wonder if she'd like to go to the mall tomorrow. - She wondered.

Her parents were supposed to be back four days from ski week.

They had decided to save their marriage, even though Marta had never believed in "heated soups", especially since she saw her mother with another man.

From a human point of view, it was really difficult to feel even an ounce of sympathy for her, but not because she was cheating on her father, but because she had lately seen her as an inconstant, sometimes envious and paranoid woman.

She was sure that she hadn't noticed her a few days earlier when she was in the car.

She was waiting for him, she realized it when she saw the man arriving a few minutes later, a man she had never seen before.

In that situation, contrary to what other teenagers angry at their mother would do, she didn't tell anyone, much less her father.

"I have to stop now, put everything in order and get into bed."

They were about to arrive, as they do every night at that hour: twenty-three and three-quarters would suddenly appear, a shadow from the mirror and then immediately afterwards another smaller one.

She didn't know what they were, but she was sure they came for her and wanted something from her.

She never thought to tell anyone, because no one would believe her.

And then here they came, fast, stealthy, dark, dark.

A hand came out of the wall, crossed the mirror and then the rest of her body made its way, it lay on the floor, slowly dragging itself towards the footboard of her bed, to go up again, floating lightly on the pink moleskin sheet, until it was on top of her, parallel to her body and only a few centimetres away from the ethereal substance it was made of.

The creature's eyes glistened as if they were made of liquid metal, black and heavy.

Marta did not move, paralyzed by terror. She could not make even a small sound, hypnotized and enraptured by the rustling of her clothes.

She looked around and remembered that she was alone, so she begged that being not to hurt her, whispering bumpy and confused words until, in the same way they had arrived, the shadows disappeared.

She talked about it only once in her family in the first period, when it all began, a few years before. She tried to inflict cuts and wounds on herself, hoping that the pain would take her away from that dark evil.

Not getting much, she switched to smoking heroin on the corners of the most hidden streets of the neighbourhood with a boy, other times within the walls of the house when her parents were at work.

The visions stopped for a few months, but her parents considered the drug to be the cause and not the remedy and locked her up for months in a clinic for psychiatric patients.

Those horrible visions were defined as nocturnal sleep paralysis, hypnagogic hallucinations, a consequence of the lack of regularity of circadian rhythms.

They put her on tranquilizers and after a few months of methadone they sent her home.

As if it was enough just a trivial tablet, a physical numbness, to heal the mortifications and dissatisfactions of the soul.

The hallucinations resumed on the very evening of her return home, when she saw the ghostly presence across the living room.

She thought it must be a kind of divine punishment and torment, deserved for having done something of which he was unaware.

Since then, she decided to stop asking questions.

"Death or these "things," sooner or later they'll come for me." She repeated her resignation to that discreet and punctual company.

"Perhaps they will put an end to this torture when I beg them to take me."

It almost seemed to her that during those temporal fractures they were waiting for a nod, a precise expression of will to death.

But she wasn't ready to die yet.

She had her paintings to finish, their music to listen to.

The next morning she took the bus to the bus stop below her house.

She waited for him for a few minutes and then saw him coming.

The driver closed the door with a smashing noise and the bus moved, roaring deafly, with sudden scrapings and singulars.

The square was silent at that hour in the greyness of a Saturday morning.

Flashes of fog enveloped the bell tower of the Matrix, you could only hear the roar of the bus and the voice of a greengrocer in the distance inviting women to buy oranges.

Her clothes were a little crumpled, but she had hidden them under a long black coat that cleverly made her stand out from the slender figure that Mother Nature had given her.

That figure, and the haughty-looking poise, had always made her look older than her age.

If by some women, like those in the alley where her grandmother lived and where she spent most afternoons after school she was admired, by her classmates she was envied and criticized: too tall, too thin or her butt too protruding.

The truth was that Marta had always been a beautiful girl and certainly did not go unnoticed among teenage girls.

The latter, humiliated by a sense of impotence to beauty, had such feelings that she was paradoxically inadequate and unworthy compared to the others.

Except for Alessandra, she was a faithful friend.

They met in kindergarten and since then they have grown up together: the same elementary school, then in middle school and high school, even in the gym.

Alessandra's house was four, maybe five kilometres away, but with a long uphill stretch heavy to do on foot.

When they were little, they often rode their bikes.

The bus suddenly nailed to the bus stop.

-Damn the brakes! - exclaimed the driver.

Finally, after a long time, she saw her friend again, visibly excited about that ride together at the mall.

Between the two girls there was affection, constant and industrious, and he was happy to see her standing up and feeling good.

She pulled out of her closet a black miniskirt that she wore with a turquoise t-shirt with little glitter that made her glow in her clumsiness as an overweight girl.

- Do you think I've lost weight? How do I look in skirts? You, on the other hand, well... you're damn skinny as a button! Are you eating?

Alessandra, among her schoolmates, was famous for her exaggeratedly worn-out speech: she could speak for more than an hour without being interrupted.

Her need to speak was so great that, in the absence of interlocutors, she was able to speak to herself in the third person.

She was that high school student who was always expected to speak.

The one the school headmaster couldn't stand and who, in school meetings, was not afraid to take the microphone and leave it until the school administration was challenged and demolished, point by point.

Marta was one of the rare people to whom, if Alessandra asked something, she would even listen to the answer. Because despite all her problems, she felt she was tied to her, for a reason unknown to her, with an invisible red thread.

She loved pass her temperas when she painted a canvas, to hear those ramblings that even her mother didn't waste any more time listening to.

She went to the kitchen and in the bowl she emptied pockets on a cabinet, took the keys to her mother's Fiesta. In Marta's company she felt more beautiful.

On the other hand, it is known that at school boys look for the alpha, the leader of the pack to feel stronger and girls the prettiest to feel more beautiful.

Their friendship was beautiful, the kind that everyone in life should remember they had in time. They always shared everything, when they had to vent, talk about a problem, do their homework or have fun, the first contact was just the best friend. And yet, because of one boy, Alessandra was put aside for a while.

He was a guy everyone knew how to use drugs, a junkie.

As a good friend, she advised her to stay away from him, but she didn't want to understand until the boy was taken away from his father. Not even the judgment of the people was able to affect the purity of such a natural and innocent feeling, that first love, even if on the other side so violent.

They headed for the mall, visited the shoe store, then a clothing store.

Finally, they went shopping at Arca, a pet shop, where Alessandra bought a pink leather collar with fake glitter for Goga, her beagle.

The girl was not used to make judgements about past events and Marta liked this: she was simply a person who could listen to another one in trouble.

They drove through the underground parking lot to get to the car when, suddenly, Marta felt a strange sensation, a sort of déjà-vu.

The round, red and green lamps above each parking space, the ones that indicate whether it is free or not, had suddenly turned all red.

The light reflected intermittently on the white border strip below had become similar to the slow motion effect of American films.

- Ale, we hadn't parked here, our parking was S3 not F8.

Even Alessandra's steps had become slower, less fluid.

A dry leaf fluttered very slowly, completely asynchronically with the wind that had pushed it upwards, a fraction of the time sequence certainly altered.

Time seemed to have stopped, but she seemed to be the only one who felt it. She turned left, saw the two shadows passing in front of her, unconsciously brushing against Alessandra and vanishing into thin air.

Once dissolved, Marta breathed again, saw the leaf hanging in the air falling on the leaden concrete at the usual speed.

Her friend turned around and asked her something she did not understand, still dazed by the vision.

It was the first time she saw them clearly outside her home, and this was enough to convince her that something horrible was about to happen.

Alessandra started the engine with a keystroke after sitting in the Audi.

- This is all wrong, something is wrong.

- What's wrong? - Asked Alessandra intrigued as they surfaced from the underground garages.

- The car was in the wrong place. First something happened in the garages and now we're in an Audi.

- Of course we're in an Audi, it's my car, don't you remember? I don't understand, what's going on?

- Your mother's car is a Fiesta, not an Audi. Pull over. We have to stop now!

- I can't pull over now, I'm cornering. Calm down and tell me what's wrong with you!

The weather was beautiful, the road was strangely lonely, the one that was always the same, travelled thousands of times in traffic was no longer so.

The car slid smoothly from corner to corner where there was supposed to be a straight.

- Stop now please, something's happening. How can you not see that?

Marta took off her seatbelt, tried to open the door but Alessandra locked it through the central controls.

- I'm sorry, I can't let you get off, I love you very much, but it's better this way. Trust me one more time.

- What's better like this? Ale...

At that exact moment, the perception of time and space was altered again.

Marta saw dazzling headlamps aimed at her friend and realized that her time was over.

In a split second, she remembered the relative definition of time and space that her philosophy professor made one day during a lecture.

"The unit of measurement of time, among the people of the ancient Near East, was the day, the month and the year. In Mesopotamia, the day began at sunset and not at sunrise, so it was the interval of time between two successive sunsets.

For this reason, when for me the day begins, I have to accept the idea that for another it ends.

It is an entirely human concept to count time, all the more so if I apply it to my personal dimension of body and spirit.

Jung once said, "Body and spirit are two aspects of the human being, and that's all we know, which is why I prefer to say that the two things happen together in a mysterious way by staying here, because you can't imagine the two things as one.

For my own use, I have conceived a principle that must show this fact of "being together", I affirm that the strange principle of synchronicity acts in the world, when certain things are produced in a more or less simultaneous way, behaving as if they were the same thing, even though they are not so from our point of view.

It was only then that I fully understood its meaning, that continuum of which the professor spoke, had been broken.

He felt the blood dripping on her face and from there it flowed on her left hand.

The acrid smoke from the airbag saturated the air in the car, and went up her nose, pinching her throat.

Alessandra's body was leaning forward, towards the steering wheel, held by the seatbelt which had probably jammed in the crash.

A woman with a strange smile was driving the other car, the one that crashed into them, and seemed to have been unharmed.

She also saw a couple of pedestrians on the road, immobile, a man and a girl who were merely observing what had happened and who did not seem to have any intention of providing any kind of assistance.

Then, nothing else.

She realized her time was over.

# 2

## *STEFANO*

Stefano Mencarini was a man of curious and lively intelligence, short black hair with a tuft that, from a young age, he never managed to keep down.

He had been married for about six years to Anna, his work colleague, and did not disdain good company and beers with friends on Saturday nights.

In short, a very ordinary man, as many can find around the world.

They hadn't had children, despite the thousands of visits made by specialists from all over Italy and all in all, he had never represented a real problem for the couple, taken as they both were by their career priorities in the biomedical engineering sector.

His life proceeded regularly, until the day he was appointed to personally oversee the opening of a new office in Havana.

He discussed it with his wife who advised him to accept the proposal.

After a few months away, the relocation would certainly have benefited their income, they could finally renovate their house, a matter always postponed for economic reasons.

Moreover, the promotion that had already been in the air for some time, would almost certainly have materialized.

So after a few weeks, he left.

Upon arrival, he realized how small José Martí International Airport was, and to an inversely proportional extent, how many mustard-colored police uniforms there were.

Obliged to go through the whole process of checking, he noticed the presence of only one detector at gate number two and realized that it would not be quick.

His high enough forehead surmounted a regular, rather handsome, but common face.

What made it special was a scar on the corner of his right eye.

It was that something lived, unique and personal. The fact that he always wore a suit and tie made a loud squeak with his appearance, to which a leather jacket would be more in tune.

An overwhelming smell of fried food rose up his nostrils, so much so that he felt as if he had gone straight into a fryer, the predominance of red present and the anachronistic structure of the building made it look like an old bus station from the fifties.

After recovering his suitcase, he changed some money into pesos, stopped in the bar near the waiting room, according to the recommendations of friends who had already been there and enjoyed that glass of rum that many found fantastic.

It was so good that it made him forget the bad smell of fried food.

Once outside the airport, he passed under yellow columns and was run over by a host of hands, arms and eyes determined to give him the keys to houses of all prices and all kinds.

Dodging them, he approached a taxi that was not far away.

He asked the sweaty man, in white shirt, to be accompanied to the hotel indicated on a business card that he showed him.

Stephen found himself with his suitcase on the edge of Plaza Vieja, opposite the entrance to a typical Cuban building of colonial architecture.

His attention was drawn to the distraught voice of a waiter on the other side of the square who was railing against some kids who were playing football and had bumped into the chairs and wrought iron table in front of his bar.

Some arches introduced him into a small alleyway paved with red bricks and framed by flowered balconies, then he passed through a very well-kept and ancient courtyard, certainly restored.

He noticed how wonderfully baroque mixed with Spanish influences before entering the lobby of his hotel.

He approached the reception desk, where a young mulatto concierge in a green suit cordially welcomed him.

He put the suitcase on the floor and handed her the papers. She went away to make photocopies, Stefano followed her with his eyes until the girl returned to the counter.

The girl gave him the key to room 28 and the documents.

- Obrigado, senhorita...Azuleya.

He thanked her, with the few words in Portuguese he knew.

She looked at him with an air of questioning, he pointed to her with his index finger the badge, pinned on the green jacket and from which you could clearly read the name.

- Oh, Claro. Or badge!

He exclaimed by touching his badge. Then she smiled and shook his hand.

- You are from Italy eu vejo. I speak your language. Nice to meet you.

He pulled the bangs out of his eyes with his hand.

- Can I help you again?

-No thanks. In fact, maybe you could set an alarm clock for me by 7:00 tomorrow morning?

- Of course, no problem. I wish you a pleasant stay at the Hotel Diaz.

When the phone rang, Stefano was awake: he
had slept poorly and badly and had attributed
the cause to rum, drunk at the airport.
His stomach seemed to be on fire.
The day had to start anyway, he decided to have
a coffee at the hotel bar and headed for a taxi,
called by the receptionist on duty.
The representative office was not far away.
That morning, he met with the engineers
selected on site, felt the ground, trying to figure
out what the real potential of these young
people was and how it could be deployed in
view of the new trade route.
He drew up an initial timetable for the training
of new recruits.
In the evening he returned to the hotel
exhausted but found the big black eyes of
Azuleya, who with pleasure proposed to be his
guide the next day through the streets and alleys
of the city.
The girl was able to arouse man's curiosity as a
source of historical and folklore curiosities from
which a thirsty man can draw.
A couple of times, during the following weeks,
they found themselves drinking in the company
of some colleagues from Azuleya who, as usual,
met at the shift change at a bar not far away.
The following Saturday, Stefano found himself
with nothing to do.

A phone call to Anna, a shower and then he opted for a walk along the streets of central Havana, drawn to the music coming in through the window.

The city centre was a riot of colour, young street musicians cheered the passers-by.

In the afternoon he visited the old town and its fortifications, remnants of its glorious Spanish colonial past for over four hundred years.

Passionate about history, he did not fail to notice the preponderance of indigenous influence linked to local building requirements and how that very resistance made them unique and very special monuments.

He returned to his hotel late at night, after staying in one of the many jazz bars scattered throughout the city, packed with tourists despite having stayed away from the larger and more famous ones.

Back at the hotel, he met Azuleya again.

They chatted for almost an hour, about everything he had seen and the many tourists present in that season.

- If you want to know the real Cuba, you have to get away from the center. Tomorrow morning, when I get off, you can come with me to Santa Maria, the village where I live. Expect only so much "Cubanity", the real one, the one that is not seen by tourists. And don't think about renting a car, we'll take the bus.

The heat was suffocating on that vehicle, even though it was nine o'clock in the morning, air conditioning not even talking about it.

The seats were anchored to the floor with nails larger than those that would actually be needed, the old driver started singing the popular songs that came out of a small radio that he kept strictly resting on his legs.

Azuleya's green uniform had given way to a white blouse and black pants.

The big dark eyes seemed to reach deep inside him, scrutinize him, analyse him finely and understand him.

Stefano noticed that she was wearing a bracelet on her wrist with a medal, he took her hand to look at it better.

- I am of the Yoruba religion. This is Yemaya, Mother of Life and Lady of the Sea. - She explained.

- I guessed she was a Virgin Mother because of the veil on her head. But why is she holding a machete? She asked.

- She likes to hunt and handle the machete, she's indomitable and cunning. The elders of the village invoke her harsh punishments and her terrible anger in their prayers, when they want her to be the executioner for some wrong at once. But she is also a sweet mother who listens to her children's demands and cares about their catch. Catholics worship her as the Virgin of the Rule. -

- That's interesting. This is the first I've heard of a Virgin Mother with a machete. - She hinted at a laugh - It's true, you'll find it's a custom.

After about thirty minutes, the bus stopped near a rusty road sign, at the crossroads of a dirt road, at the foot of which were laid provisions, and then continued on the main road.

- They are gifts, for the demons at the crossroads. But it's none of my village's business, they come from elsewhere. A few hundred metres further on, you can see a small cluster of houses, all with low roofs and coloured walls.

The first of these, along the road leading to the centre of the village of Santa Maria, had a wooden door that was very reminiscent of the old Western saloons, in dark wood with two doors.

Some small tables and chairs in white plastic were placed outside, partially shaded by a light greenish canvas stretched on reeds, like a canopy.

A skinny gentleman, with a moustache like a musketeer, asked if they would like to sit down.

- What are we having? - Stefano asked the girl, taking off his hat and putting it on the table.

- How about an ice-cold beer? I don't usually drink beer at this time of the morning, but it's pretty hot today. There's a nice microbrew. -

Azuleya nodded with her head and nodded to the bartender to approach their table, while holding on to one of the wooden doors, she dried drops of sweat from her forehead with a handkerchief.

- Oi, Nestor. Duas cervejas geladas, por favor. -

-Grandes ou pequenas? -Mm-hmm. - Precisely the hot bartender.

He placed two cork coasters on the table and placed the large dark beer mugs on them, observing the foreigner for a few seconds.

Shortly afterwards they passed in front of the ruins of some houses built by the sea, where it was evident the merciless passage of frequent hurricanes.

That point in the fishermen's bay was not spared even by the storms.

The old people of the village told how years before, there had been a violent and gigantic wave of about twenty meters that fell on that part of the coast that swept everything away.

Azuleya, a little to scare him a little to joke about it, pointed out to him that even if the sea was calm that day, one could not rule out the possibility that such a circumstance might suddenly occur.

Anyone who happened to be on the pier at that precise moment would certainly not have been able to save themselves in the face of such violence.

In fact, many had disappeared for no apparent reason or had lost their lives due to the fury of the waters.

- Unfortunately, the government no longer finances the renovation of old buildings in this area and denies permission to build new ones.

Her eyes glistened betraying a visceral love for that portion of the bay.

They continued until they reached the pretty and cozy little house of Azuleya, on an esplanade overlooking limestone cliffs.

Traditional music came down the sand dunes.

- Carmen was widowed at the age of twenty-five. Her husband, Antonio, died of illness, two years after they were married. She was already a widow when she found me on those rocks, covered only by a blue sheet, the colour of Yemaya. That's why I'm called Azuleya.

She's convinced that I came from the sea, a concession from the goddess who answered her prayer not to be alone. My birth mother never knew who she was, she certainly wasn't local, since everyone knows everything about everyone here.

- A strong, brave woman, raising you alone won't have been easy.

After making the ritual introductions and a few pleasant chats, Carmen decided it was time to give her guest a taste of the local cuisine.

Pan fried eggs, crushed fried bananas, white rice accompanied by beans and meat sauce, apart from fish and vegetables for her.

Her inquisitive gaze often reviewed the various attitudes of man, with the precise intention of finding something that didn't fit into her skin in Europe.

Among the girls of the village, in fact, were not few to have been deluded by some tourist who, once the holiday was over, abandoned them seduced and with a child.

And since she had memory of it, these kind of acquaintances were not well seen by the people of the village.

Carmen thought that her daughter was about to make the same mistake as many others and promised herself that at the end of the evening she would talk to her, to let her know how she felt about it.

She had always been a girl who was very careful with men's deceptions.

She often made friends with tourists because of the work she did, but she never took any of them to the village.

This man must have had something special. Then she noticed the wedding ring on Stefano's finger.

She thought that the wedding ring was on display and not hidden, at least it proved that he had not lied to her about his marriage.

She decided not to say anything, to trust her daughter's judgment and the fact that perhaps it was just a simple friendship.

In the afternoon the girl proposed to attend a beach party that would be held in honour of Yemaya, the village's patron saint.

Drum sounds led them among the people dancing in the streets of the small old village, a woman dressed in blue, in honour of Yemaya, opened the procession by dancing a ceremonial dance.

Her skirts were lifted up and spun rhythmically to the sound of the drums, in a crescendo of beats and, with each beat, the woman waved with movements of the torso and arms, spinning on herself.

A guide explained to the few tourists present that through the movements and swirls, the entity channelled its spirit into the priests and priestesses in trance, leaving them the message for the community.

The vigorous though simple dance fascinated the foreigners present who, mixing with the locals, began to march festively towards the fishermen's bay.

Young men stacked the wood and branches for the bonfires, previously positioned in the morning and ordered along the beach wall.

It reminded the man a little of what he saw in the French quarter of New Orleans, years earlier, during his honeymoon.

- It is very similar, this kind of party is called tongue of the saint- Azuleya explained.

- See the hourglass ones? Those are the batà drums. If you notice they have double skin, both above and below. They are each played by a drummer who places the instrument horizontally on his legs.
They are sacred instruments, they are consecrated with a secret ceremony at the end of which, the santeros, believe that the oricha Aña, master of the drums, lives inside them.
That is why all three can never be separated, placed on the ground, touched or played by women. My mother is a santera.
- You said they believe, didn't you? But what language are they singing in?
- The orichas are sung in the lucumí language, a kind of Yoruba dialect, used as the ritual language of santería.
- Yeah, but you didn't tell me if you believe it.
- I'm going dancing, are you coming? - Azuleya, he joined some of his peers and Stefano realized he shouldn't insist.
The people of the place were incredibly affectionate and hospitable, but their eyes, they showed something strange.
They looked foggy, like sick people.
He blamed it on the sun and the poor diet they were subjected to.

He learned that many of the inhabitants of the coastal villages had officially complained to the local authorities in the previous weeks about the government's ban on fish consumption, given the numerous cases of dengue in the area.

Stefano wondered how many, in the end, complied with that provision, in some ways certainly paradoxical, to the detriment of places with such a great maritime availability.

It was a strange evening.

He felt as if he were the protagonist of one of those South American telenovelas from the seventies that a local television station aired every afternoon after lunch.

In some of the scenes seen in passing, the men, all wearing big moustaches and open shirts on their chests, did nothing but drink whiskey and smoke cigars pretending to be interested in the conversations of their women, also moustached, with the air of those who only appeared in the scene. As long as they had business as a script.

Then the actors wake up and start acting.

Stefano felt precisely like a spectator, an extra, like someone who lived everything outside the scene, unable to fully penetrate the most intimate meaning of those ceremonies that for Westerners were just parties on the beach.

He sensed that there was something more spiritual than traditional costumes and folklore that only those born and raised in those places seemed to fully understand.

Especially when he saw "that something" that upset him, intent on drinking a bottle of beer lying on a blanket on the white sand.

He was lying on his side admiring Azuleya dancing among his fellow citizens.

The tongues of fire of the bonfire, now half consumed, did not allow him to have a complete view of the scene, but for a moment, it seemed to him to see her detach from the small group in absolute silence and stop in front of the sea, in the dark for a few seconds.

She walked in the sea until the water covered her head, only after several endless seconds to re-emerge and turn back.

In the meantime Stefano had hurried to meet her, worried about that long stay underwater.

She slowly resurfaced from the sea, walking towards the shore, but the colour of her eyes, from a chocolate colour, had become an intense, sparkling and unnatural turquoise.

The man stepped back a few steps, frightened and incredulous about what he was seeing, but as soon as the girl put her feet on the shore, I seemed to him the color of always. He thought that the much beer and the reflection of the light from the bonfires had played a nasty trick on him.

The next morning he found himself in a Spartan bedroom, with a big circle on his head to remind him how much he had drunk the night before.

As far as he could, he went down the stone stairs and found himself in the dining room, where the two women were busy cooking.

At that moment Azuleya's face reminded him of the kiss, a tender kiss illuminated by the vermilion reflections of the bonfires.

Not knowing how to face it, he decided not to face it at all, at least until he remembered something more precise, the alcohol vapours vanished.

They decided to return to the capital and visit the Sunday market that would be held in a historic alley near the hotel.

The main activity was concentrated in front of a shop, from where a smell of freshly baked bread came out.

Many children wandered around the neighbourhood and many beggars, any discussion could lead to violent quarrels.

Since moving, he got into the habit of "feeling the pulse" of the city, he loved to listen to that mixture of voices and accents, smells and colors.

Suddenly and effortlessly, between towels and souvenirs, everything came back to his mind: the invigorating, salty breeze hitting his face, the rhythmic lapping of the sea in the bay that brought them close to each other, when she took him by the hand, immediately after having resurfaced, the girl led him to the rocks not far away and in a ravine not visible from the beach, he made her his.

He longed for her so physically in those moments that his flesh seemed to burn that night. An inexplicable behaviour for someone like him, lucid and rational.

For the next two weeks, Stefano tried to avoid Azuleya in every way he could.

She tried several times to make contact.

Returning to the hotel, in the evening after work, he greeted her with a quick nod of his hand, not even giving her a word.

She suffered, wondering many times what she had ever said or done to receive this treatment.

In those days he heard his wife more often, trying to chase away the girl's thoughts and replace them with Anna's, repeating to himself how much she missed him, in a sort of self-conviction.

So, as in so many of the great clichés of the miserable human condition, he decided that the only sensible thing to do was to drink on it, to have the courage to start not thinking.

His mind became a blank canvas that did not allow him to think carefully about the whole thing.

In the morning he found it in his head and the more he tried to chase it away, the more his eyes and its exotic and delicate beauty stuck in his head like nails hammered violently.

Until one night the imponderable happened.

He became convinced that something had happened on the night of the bonfires, something that allowed the girl to take possession of his head.

He rushed out of room twenty-eight, crossed the corridor to the stairs that led him into the hall.

Azuleya was alone and as during all the night shifts, she allowed herself some relaxation in a room next to the reception.

He saw her with a book in her hand and her legs resting on a chair.

He threw himself at her wondering what she had done to him, pushed her against the wall and put one hand around her neck, while with the other he stroked her face heavily.

She tried to tell him something, but she couldn't pronounce that faint sound.

- What have you done to me? What kind of spell have you done to me?

- Eu não sou bruxa, I'm not a witch, I'm in love with you!

 He heard these words and trained his grip. Azuleya, completely abandoned in the grip of her embrace, bent her head backwards and, as her senses failed, he gave her the sweetest kiss.

- I will give up everything for you, everything I own and everything I am. But I will never give you up.

She didn't take his words lightly, she bent her mouth into a smile, he stared at her, making her breathe faster while a delicious thrill ran down her back.

Azuleya activated her pager and disconnected the phone, together they reached the room twenty-eight.

The resulting passion was one that few people can say they have felt, felt and touched in a lifetime.

The next day, early in the morning, they left the room together and sneakily shook hands in the crowded elevator, returning to their daily lives.

The following days they lived intensely, thinking little about it, living by moments.

On the other hand, love has nothing reasonable, it is an extraordinary adventure experienced by body and soul and compromises them both, always and in any case, irremediably.

He told her that he was going back to Italy for two weeks' holiday: she knew that he was married and that everything she was experiencing at that moment was a gift, a feeling stolen from another woman, so she didn't say a word.

Ten days went by and although she tried not to think about it too much, Azuleya reached the service room at the reception, took out her phone to put it in silent mode and slipped her purse into the top drawer of the desk.

She noticed a message from Stefano saying "think of me all day, I think of you all day."
A wide smile opened on his face, just a few days before his return.
Stefano had already built up a network of contacts in Cuba while Azuleya, although she preferred to spend every moment with him, sucked into her vortex, felt the need to go out with friends.
The love she was experiencing was totalitarian, terrified of the thought that he might leave her.
She never felt her was the other woman, but she was.
Carmen was the only one she could confide in, so one night she told her about these fears.
The saint placed a white handkerchief on her head, decorated with stones and cowries, washed her hands with apple vinegar, stood up and took a small bag of cloth from an old tin box placed on a sideboard.
She pulled out the 16 caracoles, shells that Cubans have used for centuries to receive answers from the orichas, their gods, then whispered a lullaby and threw them on the table but one fell.
According to tradition, she read twelve of them.
Suddenly her face became more serious, she looked at the girl and told her to stay away from that man.

-Minha criança, step away from this man's desire. The thirteenth shell, Metanlá, has fallen. You must stay away from him. The goddess wants something from you. To fulfil your wish she will take from you what you hold most dear.
You are a daughter of Yemaya remember, she saved you, everything you desire she will grant you.
But whatever she wants, you must give it to her.
Be careful, my daughter, because you might not like what he asks for in exchange for that man's love.

- I wrote this for you on the plane. –
He got out of bed by lifting up the crumpled sheets and headed for the jacket thrown on the back of a chair further away. He picked up a piece of paper and handed it to Azuleya who felt his heart plunge and saw the tender and frightened expression on her face.

*I'd like to find you as you walk,*
*approaching me on an alien night*
*Dream bonfire rising with the full moon,*
*the sand glistening beneath my feet.*
*A drum resounds for the daughter of the sea*
*My heart listens, your smell speaks to me,*
*in an atavistic beat desire beats.*
*Each caress can make a note,*
*in a score of desire that dares,*
*Then you finally become perfect vision*
*of turquoise nymph dancing on the loins of the sea.*

- It's beautiful, thank you. –
A tear ran down Azuleya's face.
He thought that Yemaya had surely heard his request.
They spent the night together hugging each other, and when the morning after the phone call from the reception desk woke him up, he realized that she had already left.

It had been almost two months since the bonfire party.

The two saw each other regularly, their meetings made of passion and the weekends spent at the bay of Santa Maria, made him forget the feelings of guilt towards Anna who, on the contrary, perhaps aware of an imminent separation, claimed several times with the company the definitive return to Italy of her husband.

Women's intuition is known to be formidable. Someone once said that a woman's intuition is much closer to the truth than a man's certainty.

Azuleya, she vomited all night and the next morning as understandable she couldn't get her head off the pillow.

Carmen asked her if there was a possibility of becoming pregnant, a tremor spread throughout Azuleya's body.

- He can't have children, she told me several times. He has one of those seminal fluid defects, it can't be. I certainly didn't digest dinner, Mom.

She took a little notebook out of the drawer.
- Shit, I'm late.
A few hours later, Azuleya found herself staring at the two red lines on the pregnancy test, wondering how Stefano would react.
She heard a knock on the bathroom door.
She simply said to his mother, "I'm going out."

She stayed home two days after work, then decided that sooner or later, she would have to tell Stefano.

She was convinced that at that news, he would faint with joy.

She imagined that she would continue to work until his health had allowed it without problems and that, if it was a boy, they would call him Carlo, after Stefano's father.

She also thought about his wife, how she would react to the news and decided not to put herself in his shoes.

One thing was never in question for her: she would follow that man to the end of the world.

The next morning, she woke up with a light breeze that slightly moved the macramé and beaded curtains hanging from the window panes, making them clink.

In addition to the usual scent of the sea and coffee, prepared by Carmen, who climbed the stairs like every morning, an acrid rotten smell disturbed her.

She got up and looked out of the window and saw the leaves of the old twisted trees and the hedges of the small garden shining a deep green.

The rock of the sea lilies was already immersed from dawn in the blue heat, looking lighter and lower.

On the other side of the bay, the small river glistened like a winding stream of liquid mercury before diving into the sea.

Azuleya thought the story of the pregnant woman's sense of smell was true.

They say it worsened considerably during the early stages of pregnancy.

She heard an annoying buzz of flies on the now rotten fruit box, leaning on the garden chair, waiting to be bagged and placed with all the other junk outside the entrance gate, where it would be picked up by the picker.

She got dressed and after having had coffee and yogurt, her stomach was grateful.

On arrival at the hotel she met Stefano, said goodbye to each other and made an appointment for eight o'clock in her room.

And so it was.

The man hugged her and began to caress her.

- Wait, please wait. I have something to tell you, or rather show it to you.

Stephen, intrigued, couldn't help but notice a peculiar smile on his face.

- It must surely be something beautiful. -

-Have a seat. I have something to give you. –

The girl pulled out of the bag next to her, the test case. - Look.

Stephen's smile became a strange grimace of surprise.

He knew very well that tool, he had held it in his hand many, many times and as many times he had remained staring at that one disappointing red line, while Anna dried her eyes.

This time it was different.

Azuleya tried to keep smiling, but her standing still, turning the test in her hands, terrified her. It wasn't the reaction she expected.

Stephen's gaze remained fixed and low on the two vertical lines for a few very long seconds.

- I'm pregnant, not invisible. Say something, please. Stephen stood still.

- How was this possible?

- Well, do you want me to explain how babies are born? - replied Azuleya, in a tone of voice that was irritated by those long awaited words.

-Hey, what do you want me to say, I'm married, or have you forgotten?. What do you expect me to do, jump for joy? - He got out of bed and nervously walked around the room.

-Damn it. You want me to call her and tell her, you know, dear, you know that girl I'm fucking in Cuba? Well, she's pregnant now. Isn't that what you'd like?

- Asshole, fuck you. - She was so fucking irate.

At those words, she understood that the matter would certainly not take the turn she had imagined, she grabbed her bag and went out.

Azuleya, once home, told everything to Carmen who reminded her of the warnings given by the Caracoles.

- You wouldn't listen to the spirits. This story will end badly for you, you'll see. –

Two days went by and on the phone, finally a message from Stefano. "Meet me tonight. We need to talk."

She waited for him in his room for about ten minutes.

He sat down in the white wooden chair, knees parallel and tight.

She twisted her fingers for a while, then put them on the table the moment he heard the door open.

Stefano went to meet her, gave her a kiss on the forehead and asked her if she wanted something to drink.

When she refused, he grabbed a chair and sat by her side.

- I've thought a lot about the situation, you know. I love you, but you must understand that I have a wife in Italy who I would never hurt, for anything in the world.

- Sure, because you didn't hurt her by sleeping with me, did you? You didn't hurt her just because she doesn't know? - She broke it off.

- I didn't say that. Anna and I built a space, a world of our own, where there's a place for everything and everything's in place. You are the other, the freedom, the passion, the escape that makes me appreciate life. A fatherhood I can't handle and maybe I don't want to, not without you.

We've wanted a child so much that I can't imagine having one that excludes her, after what we've suffered. It would mean betraying her twice. There's nothing left to do but have an abortion.

Stefano, never in his life, saw such a load of bitterness and disappointment in someone's eyes. He felt himself dying inside for a moment, his heart full of beats until a few minutes before, now it was silent.
The girl got up so fast.
- What? The truth is that I've been a pastime for you. You talk about her and you don't even care about me or this child. You're a selfish man and a liar, I was wrong to fall in love with you.

The words came out of her mouth like they were waiting for nothing else to happen.
He was a man she didn't recognize and above all didn't like, while he tried to say something, she froze him with a frown. She looked at him the last time, but as if it was the first time. Because for the first time she looked him straight in the face, without lowering her gaze.
- I'm gonna do what's right. From this moment on, neither I nor the child is anymore of your business, don't you dare ask me to do anything, let alone look for me, you have no right. Goodbye, Stefano. –
The man remained thinking, motionless in that position for a long time.
He thought about what marriage to Anna was, what it had become. But then it was said to be normal, it happened to all married couples, when passion became camaraderie in a quiet and lasting affection.

Even if men needed an adventure from time to time, a wife would always remain a wife.

The next morning, Azuleya came home after the night shift, ran to her room without saying a word to her mother, who inexplicably or simply by intuition, understood everything.

Carmen joined her in her room, sat on the bed and the girl's head found comfort on her knees.

She cried. The mother didn't speak, she just wiped away her tears.

Too much importance is attached to words, and Carmen knew, as a wise woman, that sometimes one must remain silent to take on another person's pain.

- And now what? - Whispered Azuleya.

- Now you'll go on as you've always done, Yemaya's daughter. You'll live your abandoned life again. Why wouldn't you listen to me? But this time you won't have only me.

Stefano left after two days, determined never to return to Cuba.

He embraced his wife again, leaving the girl from the bay behind him.

It is well known that the distance after a while, putting out the small fires and feeding the big ones, and inside himself, what at first seemed an easy and necessary sponge bath, turned out to be the greatest pain and condemnation he had ever felt.

Until, six months later, he felt the lucid awareness of a mistake that soon became remorse, torment and dismay for what he had done. He tried to call Azuleya several times, but his phone number was always unreachable. She had probably changed her number.
He then tried to contact the hotel, but he was told that she had resigned some time before.
He was convinced that she had done so in order to erase any landmarks he could use to track her down. She never wanted to be found.
His pride lay overwhelmed, he opened a dispute with himself, marvelling at how he could have made that very mistake, as if only part of himself was responsible for it, and he wanted to disown that part forever.
After some time, a letter arrived with a picture of a very small girl.
"In spite of everything, this is Stella. She was born on August 10th, the night of St. Lawrence.
"She weighs three and a half kilos and is beautiful."
Stefano closed that letter and hid it in the last drawer of his desk, inserted between folders of documents, archived.

# 3

## *GRETA*

They rang the door.
Suddenly a subtle rivulet of anguish crept between Greta's shoulder blades.
She barely moved, staggering and managed to reach the door.
She expected to see the police, but it was Stella, hes opposite.
- You have to come with me now. - She said agitated.
At that moment she turned her head and saw a boy from upstairs coming up the stairs. She hesitated for a moment, looking at him. "What a busybody," she thought.
She grabbed her jacket and followed her into the garage.
There was a red sign on the wall of her parking space that literally plunged her into an abyss of terror.

**I KNOW WHAT YOU DID.**

Her legs didn't support her and she fell sitting on the frozen concrete in the garage.
Stella helped her up and held her arm and walked her to her apartment.

- We've known each other for many years. - She told her as he helped her sit on the sofa - Tell me what happened, if I can help you, I will. –
She decided to trust her and tell her everything, she felt a great need to ease her conscience, but Stella interrupted her.
- The first thing we have to do is erase that inscription. - She said in a peremptory tone. - I've got some white paint at home, and with the brush in ten minutes you can cover it up. Don't worry. You'll tell me all about it later, okay? -
Greta was in too violent a state to keep quiet.
  -I'm not worried about the writing.
-I'm more worried about someone trying to pin it on me. For God's sake! Someone saw me that night! It has entered after me there is no other explanation.
He was killed and what more absurd, I have made everything easier having handcuffed him to the bed.
But I didn't kill him, trust me! I wish I had, but I didn't.
- I told you later. Go take a shower and calm down. You'll explain everything later, I have to hurry now. Do you want someone to see that writing?
Stella went out and closed the door behind her.

Greta took a shower, put on her pyjamas and her thoughts went to the boy who had hesitated a moment before continuing along the stairs. What if it had been him? She tried to remember his features but she never saw him in the building.

After a few minutes, she heard the door across the street open.

She looked out on the landing, Stella had returned.

- It's okay... give me a minute to put this stuff away and I'll be right with you.

Greta's kitchen clock read 2:00. The two women found themselves sitting on the sofa.

-I don't know where to start.

- Start at the beginning, it'll be easier to get to the bottom of the whole mess

Stella listened without interrupting, thinking only about how much she had changed.

The woman who was in front of her at that moment, was completely different: fragile and confused, she was certainly not that smug and rigid chopstick that a few months before she didn't even speak to her.

The loss of her daughter Marta had been a hard blow for her, of those who break down the most solid mental dams.

And how the waters, at first subtracted from their natural course and channelled into constructed paths made of appearances, resistance and lies, at the moment she gave in overwhelmed and revealed all the weaknesses and frailties of her being.

She understood that Greta had always lived in fiction. Her whole life was a fiction starting with her marriage. And it was precisely there that she began to tell the story in detail.

- One morning I woke up with an annoying ray of sunshine in my eyes. I was still sleepy, but I realized it wasn't my home.

My temple was throbbing at the same rhythm as the minute hand of a clock on the wall, and I saw clothes on the floor.

I squinted a little trying to focus and recognized a grey man's shirt on the floor that brought me back to the night before.

Yes, Stella, I was cheating on my husband with a high school friend, Stefano, found after twenty years. He, married and childless, handsome, successful man, and I... what?

You know, I met Marco before the end of the second year of university and I got pregnant almost immediately. Pervaded by the enthusiasm and passionate euphoria of the beginnings we found ourselves, from one month to the next, we were taking care of a daughter, Marta.

Despite the love I felt for her, I always felt stuck in a life I didn't want to live.

Oh, man! I shouldn't have washed greasy, dusty mechanic's overalls. It wasn't the life I dreamed of.

Always the same days marked by the usual hours, the usual things, the usual engagements. I swear they were wearing me down from the inside out.

- We all have a past we don't like. In many circumstances, I too would have liked and should have been more sincere, more brilliant, more honest, more decisive. Over time, it's easy to say something like that.

- I'm going to make some tea.- I foresee a long night of confessions.

She laid Stella out, smiling.

In recent years the girl had learned that life is never static.

Neither are feelings.

The only solution she found possible when she found herself in such a situation before was change: change alone or change with her partner, but never stand still.

If we remain passive and immobile, she thought, life will choose for us and that is when we will have to prepare for everything, even a tsunami.

And Greta's tsunami was called Stefano.

- I don't know, if you've ever noticed a man's eyes when he finds you interesting. Those eyes that look at a woman and can do everything, keep you in check, making you feel the most beautiful, the most desired. Stefano used to look at me like that, like he hadn't looked at his wife in years.

I thought he hated her the way he talked about her, or he couldn't forgive her anything.

Probably, he couldn't forgive himself for something he'd done in the past, I don't know. Then that feeling of pleasure, infinite pleasure, that pleasure mixed with transgression that I had never felt with Marco in twenty years of marriage.

I never felt guilty, he deserved it. He never made me feel like that, never.

Lately I only felt a feeling of disgust when he kissed me.

He noticed it but he preferred to pretend it was nothing, until I put an end to it all, taking a break by mutual agreement and he moved in to his mother. –

Greta took a sip of tea, then continued.

- The first time we met at my house, Marta was at her father's. I still have him in front of me repeatedly feeling the tie knot with his fingers, sitting on the sofa while I was making a coffee. He seemed perfect to me. He was perfect, in his black suit and red tie, while he was looking around.

I saw his gaze resting on a picture of me in his twenties, leaning against a corner of the black and white wall bookcase, and he stood up to take it. I asked him to join me in the kitchen, put the coffee in the cups and put it back.
He stood in front of me and started talking about the cause. Then you know what I did?
I stood in front of him and told him I was tired of hearing talk, I had other plans for how to spend the night.
I followed the silhouette of the tie all the way down his shirt, then I stroked his chest and he kissed me.
The new Greta had got the better of the old, demure Greta, I guess he didn't expect it.
A smile was printed on his face as he looked me in the eye.
I told him to undress by biting his earlobe, he took off his jacket and I loosened my tie. He caressed my cheek with the back of his hand. The thing that excited me the most in that situation was the fact that I had surprised him, he was serious and sure of himself, who had hesitated for a moment, before I understood what I wanted.
Those blue eyes... blue, blue eyes, surrounded by long dark eyelashes peering at me, not knowing how far he could go.
We spent the night together, one of the most satisfying nights of my life.
The next morning I woke up at six.

I wondered if I had just been dreaming, but seeing the red tie dangling from the white wrought iron back, I realized that it had all really happened the night before. I found a note on the sheets next to the pillow:
Thank you for a wonderful night. I'm sorry I won't wake up next to you after tonight.
I was happy and finally free to live playfully.
But one thing struck me about that man: that underlying melancholy that only those who have experienced pain possess, and those who possess it can recognize it when they see it in another person.
We went on dating for a while.
One Thursday I saw him arrive as beautiful as an Adonis.
I was in front of the hotel where we used to get a room, on Thursday afternoons, not far from his office.
Suddenly I felt the presence of someone behind a car parked out front.
The arrival of Stefano distracted me from that distraction, inviting me to come up to the house.
Now I know who was spying on us, and I'm so sorry. But Marta knew what fucking love was!
She had already experienced it, she couldn't conceive the idea of being without that vile being that had torn her heart to pieces several times, how could she judge me?

One day I came home early from work and found her in her room, with a knife in her hand while she was pulling small pieces of flesh from her arms, she touched the top of depression a few months later, when she told me about strange hallucinations and, under the advice of the doctors, we hospitalized her in a special structure.

It wasn't my fault, Marta was fragile, it wasn't up to me or my actions.

She was weak! All I could do was bring her canvases and colours, the only things that brought a minimum of activity into her life.

Canvas after canvas, her subject was always the same: still life. She hadn't fully recovered, but a few months later she returned home. Do you know what she was able to do? To advise her father to mend the relationship with me and that there was something wrong with the way we led them.

Marco then booked a skiing holiday in Courmayeur in a chalet, the typical mountain hut.

But who asked him? Why did She interfere in my life? -

- You loved her and you had your reasons for doing what you did, surely. –

Stella, put her hand to her forehead whispering that the woman was much more messed up than she thought.

- Before Marta's death, I was swallowing sedatives that not only kept me from sleeping, but also prevented me from thinking quickly about where I had gone wrong with her.
After her death I didn't take them anymore, I wanted to be lucid and present to myself.
The truth is that I didn't need them anymore.
 Things were worse between my husband and me.
We had both changed who in one way and who in the other, but while he found the strength to go on because of my closeness, I could not.
I had some difficult nights, terrible nightmares, but on the other hand I had lost some weight and I was physically magnificent. I had always been maybe, but I never realized it.
I really liked myself: when I looked in the mirror I found myself beautiful, long legs that I liked to caress myself in front of the mirror, the still firm breasts that I discovered little by little, just as I discovered and enjoyed the pleasure of a new me.
The thing that drove me crazy was the look in men's eyes when I walked, whether on the street or in the supermarket or in the office.
I may seem degenerate to you, but since my daughter's death I've been reborn, stronger than before. Do you know how I ended it with Stefano? - She asked Stella.
- I have no idea. - She answered by showing her palms.

- As quickly as possible. I saw him as a wimp at that point.

He confided in me once that he hated his wife for taking him away from a probably happier life, just for the semblance of morality and social obligation.

He too was a man without character and I didn't know what to do with him.

One night we were lying on the bed hugging each other for a long time and suddenly I simply told him that it was over and that we should never see each other again.

He didn't move and didn't speak, I got up, put on my shoes and without looking back I took my bag on the floor near the closet and left.

I knew I'd never see him again. I couldn't carry on that relationship, I was enough for myself now.

I had that clarity of mind that is hidden in everyone no matter what moves around them.

My liberation was to have the knowledge that I was bargaining with memory a period of oblivion from memory.

It's strange to describe, but I felt a stronger and more inexplicable desire to get out, to meet new people, to live.

Do you know what I did one night?

One night, wandering around the streets of the city, I decided to stop at a big bar table and get something warm.

I noticed a guy sitting at a table with a cup of coffee and an open newspaper in front, a worker I suppose, given the reflective vest he was wearing.

He stood up and came towards me, I remember not having heard a word out of his mouth, I saw only his lips moving, then I took him by the hand, without speaking I took him in my car, in the dark parking lot at the back of the bar.

The boy went right out of his mind when I unbuttoned the top of my blouse.

He pulled a condom out of his pants and we had sex, with a lust I didn't know was part of me until then.

And it finally came out, the Greta hidden for decades, the real me.

The weirdest thing is that her face kept changing during sex. -

- How did it change? – Stella, curious, asked.

- I don't know how to explain it. Every time I looked at him he seemed like a different person, as if he wore multiple faces to hide his true identity.

With every glare of light, every detail of him was new to me.

I understood why one night's adventures for so many are a simple way to satisfy the desire for a fleeting yet fulfilling connection.

A way to protect yourself from being vulnerable and susceptible to the influence and power of others, concentrating and enjoying only that transgression. The boy handed me his number written on a piece of paper and I threw it in the first dumpster.

The next day, during my lunch break, I stopped in front of a shop window where the tattoo sign stood out brightly.

I came out with a phoenix tattooed all over my back. It was a symbol of my rebirth.

The adventure with the guy in the bar left me with a feeling of omnipotence, I felt that something had happened, a change I would never have thought before.

The detachment from reality and affection was complete, I decided that I would no longer suffer.

- I understand you, and I'm not judging you. I know what it's like to be alone.

Stella got up, took the cups from the coffee table and brought them into the kitchen by placing them in the sink.

Then she looked out the living room door and showed her a cigarette waving it between her fingers.

- I'm going to smoke a cigarette on the balcony. - Greta nodded.

The moon was high in the sky and veiled by a light fog, the air was cold because of the time. Stella squeezed herself in her shoulders and thought about when after Marta's death, Greta called her to help her in the house with the cleaning.

- Now I want you to tell me what that sign in the garage means. –

She asked her to close the french window.

- Okay. One day I was in the office, I remember I had a headache so bad, so much to see blurry.

"Greta shortly will be arriving the counterparty lawyer to try an out-of-court settlement. You should hold off until the end of the meeting."

The boss told me.

Since it was already 6:00, I resigned myself to being late that evening.

The first person to enter the room was a young, goggle-eyed lawyer, I showed him the door of the firm where the meeting was to be held and a few minutes later his client arrived, who introduced himself as Gianni Serra.

I invited him to follow me and enter in the office.

The next day I saw this Gianni again, he came to bring a certificate to attach to the file the day before and to let Lorenzo know.

He was a handsome man, well dressed and with a very pleasant perfume, sandalwood I think.

He asked me if I was free for my lunch break and if he could offer me something to drink with the excuse of explaining the agreement, signed the night before.
I said yes, that I'd be off at half past one, then back to work an hour later.
We could meet directly at the diner under the office where I used to stop.
I remember getting a steak that was unsalted, undercooked. It was disgusting, he had a couple of chicken legs with a side of roast potatoes.
"What's your name? Or should I keep calling you ma'am," he said with a cheeky little smile.
We spent half an hour talking about the lawsuit he was involved in, too.
We said goodbye and I went back to work.
I didn't hear from him for a couple of days, until he came into the office to talk to the lawyer.
He asked if he could have my number so he could have a word with me once in a while.
I gave it to him and he left.
One night I took my computer, snooped around on the internet, read some news stories, then the last big billionaire divorce of a couple of American actors and ended up opening my Facebook profile.
After a few seconds, I got a message in Gianni's chat room saying hello and asking me how my day went.

I remained doubtful for a moment about his intentions, I didn't know what to answer. Then, after a few unimportant chats, he asked me if I wanted to have dinner with him the following Saturday, in friendship, he would introduce me to his wife. I was unsettled a little at first, but I decided to accept the invitation.

He told me that it would be a special feast and that a bit of fun would help take my mind off my daily worries.

That Saturday night I took a long time to choose what to wear and in the end, I opted for a black sheath dress on the knee of the classic ones, a very good ally of women who don't want to make mistakes.

His house was actually a secluded villa that had the outside gate open on the driveway in front of the villa.

I thought he was a very rich man, I went in welcomed by a waiter.

I left my coat to him and headed in the direction of Gianni who called my attention from the salon.

There were about ten people present and after the pleasantries, I took a glass of prosecco on a tray.

I understood from the jokes and speeches made that Gianni was an entrepreneur in banking and real estate.

His young blonde wife, Olga, invited me to follow her on a sofa, told me about her life and how she had arrived in Italy.

She was a model in Ukraine and that didn't surprise me but I wondered how she ended up in a villa with an old rich man.

She was really beautiful.

She had a very particular and elongated, almost oriental, ice-blue eye cut and two kilometres long legs.

I asked her how she met Gianni.

She admitted, very candidly, that one of her agents had proposed her as an escort for a business trip to Russia, where she would also act as an interpreter.

The term escort confused me a little bit.

I asked her if she was an interpreter but she answered very naturally: "No, I was an escort, a whore."

I didn't know what to say, I was stunned by such frankness.

I went back to their house several times, from then on a beautiful friendship was born.

Until that damn evening, when Olga called me and said: "We have to talk, Gianni wants to see you.

Tonight at seven o'clock he's waiting for you at the Blue-sky bar, the one near the bus station".

I wondered what had happened for making that strange request.

I sat down at a table and ordered a spritz.

It was a suburban bar, not one of the nice and modern ones, but it was more of a meeting place for old people who played cards.

A small, fat woman in a blue scrubs was pushing a bucket out of the bathroom with her foot, and she kept passing the mop on the floor.

The smell of the detergent she was using bothered me a lot. My attention was drawn to a painting on the walls that had a light wood frame, I focused my eyes ajar and noticed that the subject was the interior of a hospital, with blurred details.

I wondered who, among people with a minimum of good taste, could have attacked such a painting in a bar.

Gianni arrived apologizing for the delay and sat down in the chair in front of me.

He asked the guy behind the bar for a prosecco, apologized for wanting to meet me like that and needed to talk to me face to face about something important.

He said he'd arranged a dinner the following Saturday and would also invite a big shot from the Vatican.

A cardinal, a corrupt "piece of shit" as he called him, who was putting a dear friend of his in trouble by not wanting to sign a concession on land owned by the Church of Rome.

I asked what I could do.

He told me that he was going to mount a micro-camera on a handbag, the very small and almost invisible ones, and that I would have to seduce him in some way, so as to allow the recording of the meeting and be able to hold him with blackmail.

I immediately said no, that Olga could have done it. In short, to cheat the men who have ruled Rome and the whole world for centuries, did not make much sense to me.

He explained to me that I should only "create" a situation that could compromise him publicly. I told him: I don't know Gianni... I mean, would he notice? Then you're assuming that he likes me enough to take me to a hotel or home", I told him. Shit, that was a high prelate we were talking about, a man of God.

He assured me he wouldn't back down by being a whoremonger.

Olga had known him for years and he certainly wouldn't fall for it.

He told me that the fact that she asked me such a favour was a sign of what and how much he trusted me. -

Stella listened to that last part with her grainy eyes, then avoided interrupting it.

Puffing, she brought her hand to her mouth, almost stopping it.

Greta continued.

- On the evening of the dinner I arrived on time and Gianni welcomed me into the usual dining room. -

- I had never paid attention to the valuable furniture in the house before, I was also struck by a wall device, a sort of electronic panel, whose subjects changed according to the music it was playing.

He looked for a small remote control that he found on a dark wooden sideboard and after pressing a button, some lyrical music reached my ears with perfect acoustics.

It seemed to come from all directions.

There were two other people in the house I had never seen before, to whom I showed my bag, to mount the micro-camera.

They explained that I should just put it on a table or a piece of furniture and it would record everything.

Gianni reassured me, even at the last minute I could change my mind and nothing would happen.

The sound of the intercom, shortly after, interrupted our conversation while a maid was bringing canapés and aperitifs to the table.

Gianni went to the door and then returned to the room with two men who seemed to have a lot of confidence in him.

The guests apologized for the delay and, after the presentations with the other diners, took their seats at the table.

I had recognized one of them, I had seen him in the office a few years before.

I felt a twinge in my temple, which fortunately passed quickly.

The Honourable in the Cardinal's company didn't recognize me and I pretended nothing when they introduced us. I tried to flirt a little with the Monsignor during dinner, to see if he was attracted to me in the first place.

He was a fat, arrogant little man, one of those characters who looked like he'd come out of a comic book artist's pencil, with a button nose and a mouth too wide for his face.

Gianni, at the end of the evening, looked at me with the look of someone waiting for a nod, an answer, I said yes with a nod of my head.

At that point I approached the cardinal and asked him if he had the pleasure of having a drink with me after dinner.

In his eyes, I was certainly like one of the many social climbers, one of those women susceptible to the halo of charm that power sometimes creates.

He greeted the owner of the house, then exchanged a few words with the man with whom he had arrived, and finally invited me into the car.

"I'd rather follow you in mine, if you don't mind." I told him.

We headed towards a seaside resort not far away and once we arrived I parked a little further away from the front door.

It was the classic summer holiday cottage, with palm trees and umbrellas closed on top of aluminium and canvas deckchairs, as you can see a lot of them, then he made his way inside the apartment.

He invited me to sit on the leather sofa, took a bottle of wine and two glasses and sat next to me. He began to take an attitude that a woman can recognize very well: from his gestures, from his words and from the gullible interpretations of himself, all the cowardice dictated by advantage shone through.

A dirty seduction that he used as a strategy aimed at the here and now of those who want to "own" for the time of a night, those that in the morning, would leave him with a feeling of narcissistic and refined complacency of his own person and qualities, with the illusion of being a span above all other men on Earth.

He never had, and could never have had, any kind of effect on me.

It had always been the synthesis of the clichés of everything I hated in a man, not to mention betrayal of a God he had sworn to serve.

He first put his hand on my knee, then approached me in the hope of giving me a kiss on the lips, but I managed to dodge him.

He took off his cassock and placed the solid gold cross on the tea table.

At that moment, I felt the last semblance of respect that was due to him for what he stood for.

I felt his hands on my thighs and felt disgust, I pushed him away.

Smiling and winking, I asked him to wait for me in my room while I went to the bathroom to freshen up.

I locked myself in and tried to breathe and calm down, I should have placed the camera so that it would record him undressing and I should say or do something compromising, then I would back out.

I got up my nerve and as I came out I heard him calling me from a room upstairs.

I took off my shoes and left them at the bottom of the stairs made of a nice, ice-coloured, mottled marble.

In my hand I felt the cold of the dark metal of the handrail, I walked towards the upper floor from which came the sound of stale chamber music, like the cardinal.

Looking around, I saw a spot in the chest of drawers that was placed on the wall next to the bed that seemed to be the perfect place to put the bag and give a good view of the room to record the meeting.

He was on the bed in his boxer shorts trying to tear a page out of a Bible and roll it up to snort a strip of cocaine.

Just the shot of that moment would have been enough but I wanted to be more than sure to record a few more frames that could serve the purpose.

Slowly but casually I took my clothes off, standing in front of the bag in my bra and thong, approached him and straddled him, swayed a couple of times with my pelvis and decided that it would be enough.

He looked at me astonished and asked me what I was doing.

For a few seconds he was petrified, then I told him I was sorry but I wasn't feeling very well and I was going home.

He yelled at me and said, "Why are you leaving me like this? Where can I find a whore at this hour?"

All I remember is that I picked up the bag and ran out to the car, came home satisfied and lightened by the weight of that fiction. I took a shower on the fly and put on a jumpsuit, decided to check the video, but there wasn't even a trace of the camera in the bag.

I thought I dropped it on the way to the car and went back to the cottage to look for it.

I noticed a comings and goings of police cars along the road, I thought of an accident, but the police were going out of the house of the pig where until a few hours before I was present too.
I thought about what the hell might have happened.
That he'd been sick? At that point I asked a policeman who was standing a few yards from the door, and he told me that a man had been murdered in his house.
I felt faint, walked around looking for the micro-camera without being noticed. Nothing. There was no trace of it. -
Greta got up and took a glass, poured herself some whisky that she found inside a piece of furniture.
She offered Stella a glass, which she refused.
- Fuck!
 Stella got up and started walking around the room nervously.
Then she approached her and said in a reassuring tone:
-Listen to me, there's no point in despairing like this now.
The micro-camera sure didn't find it. Think about it. If they'd seen the footage, they'd be here already.
Just because you've been to her house doesn't mean you're a murderer. If you're questioned, you'll tell the truth, that you had a drink at his place and left right afterwards. -

She walked over to the sink, filled a glass of water and swallowed it all at once. Then she went back on: - Greta, it'll be fine, you'll see. Now go rest. Tomorrow you'll go to the police and talk to them spontaneously. If they ever find the micro-camera, you'll tell them everything. -

- I could say from the start that to resume was a game proposed by the cardinal and that at a certain point, I changed my mind and left. -

She said goodbye to Stella, then after a while she collapsed exhausted in his sleep so much sought after.

She decided that when she woke up, she would phone Gianni. Greta rested only at times, thinking of the risk she was taking.

These and other questions tortured her for much of what was left of the night until the next morning.

She called Gianni and he reassured her that she would hear from a friend of hers who worked at the police station to find out more and so she did.

After about twenty minutes she called back from an unknown number.

- Greta, his throat was cut.

They found him on the bed, in a lake of blood.

I asked if they made any guesses about what could have happened, who could have done such a thing.

My friend told me that the police are beating the lead on prostitution and drugs, since they found several doses of cocaine in the house. But rest assured, they don't have anything that can lead back to you. -

- Gianni, there's a problem. The micro-camera's gone. I lost it. - He confessed.

His voice, quite firm and reassuring enough until my admission, betrayed an inclination in tone, a small variation that denoted a growing restlessness.

On the other hand, she knew very well the risk she would take as the principal of the making of that video.

She decided to call Stefano, the only one who might be able to help her.

The answering machine took that little hope away from her. She was unreachable.

At that point, she felt she could only count on Stella, that last-minute ally you don't expect.

She could never win that battle alone.

On closer inspection, she thought maybe Gianni was right to say they had nothing on her.

She heard a very loud knock on the door, looked at the clock at eight o'clock.

Greta rushed to the door thinking it was her, ignoring that it might be two policemen standing in front of her.

- Ma'am, there's an urgent summons if you don't mind following us. -

- About what? Sorry, did something happen?

She asked, pretending to be surprised by that visit and trying to fix his robe.

- I'm sorry, I can't tell you anything specific. We only have orders to accompany you immediately to Inspector De Simone. He will explain everything. - The eldest of the two specified.

- I have to get dressed, as you can see I'm still in my pyjamas. Give me a few minutes. In the meantime, sit down in the kitchen.

She picked up the phone and called Stella.

Evidently she had already gone out because she didn't answer, so she quickly wrote her a message informing her of what was happening.

They made sat her in a waiting room in front of the inspector's office, the policemen entered a room and after a few seconds they came out with a middle-aged man, bearded and wearing glasses, who signaled her with two fingers to come in.

The man stood at the door and led her into the office.

- Please, have a seat. - he said pointing to the chair.

- Why am I here? Has something happened to my husband? -

- No, ma'am, he's here because he needs to answer a few questions. –

He said in a dry tone while opening a ring binder.

- Tell me about it. -

- Do you know Cardinal Tanzi Barbuti? -

- Yeah, sure. Why? - She asked, pretending to be surprised.

- Well, His Excellency was found murdered in his home with five shots fired from the inner shaft of a large candle holder, one of which was to the femoral artery which was fatal. How long since you've seen him? -

To this question, she remembered what Stella told her: "If they ask you about him they know you were there, so you have to tell the truth."

She decided to answer completely truthfully.

- I saw him at a friend's house two nights ago, during a dinner at Gianni Serra's house. -

- A dinner at Gianni Serra's house? Gianni Serra who, the real estate agent? –
He turned in amazement to one of the policemen who, meanwhile, entered the room.
- Well, he usually hangs out at his house. We're friends. I haven't known him long. Excuse me, but why exactly am I here? –
- Ma'am, they killed a cardinal we know was a dinner companion at a dinner party you attended the other night. –
He turned to get a pen and a piece of paper from a colleague behind him.
- Write down the address of this Serra. And please write the name of those present at the dinner on this paper. - He continued, handing her the black pen after tapping it regularly against the desk.
- Come on, you know who the others were.
She answered.
The man shook his head, wrinkling his eyebrows, as Greta began to write.
- Now tell me everything, in detail.
Can you also tell me what time you left and how? Did someone take you home, or did you go home alone?
- I was leaving but on the door the cardinal asked me if I wanted to have a drink with him.
- And did you go?
De Simone started tapping the pen on the desk again.

Greta thought it was one of the many techniques that cops use to make those they are interrogating nervous, and maybe, make them fall into contradiction.
She tried to isolate that annoying noise.
- Yes, I followed him in my car because I was tired, so I could get home as soon as possible on my own. I thought he was stopping at some bar, but instead he headed towards the coast, so much so that I got a little angry.
- Why did you get angry?
He asked her in a moment of silence.
She tried to calibrate as well as she could, for fear of reporting more than she really needed, without compromising her.
- Because I thought there were plenty of pubs or drinking establishments to go to.
I don't like to drive at night and I was already predicting the return, along that dark road.
In fact, I was about to pull over and call him and tell him I was coming home when I saw the arrow flashing to turn.
- So what happened next?
He asked her, looking her in the eye.
The inspector had finished reading the pages in the binder and focused exclusively on the woman.
Greta tried to collect every shred of self-control she possessed.
She took a deep breath.

-Nothing, he offered me a glass of wine, we talked for about half an hour or so, after which I went home. That was it.

De Simone went towards the window, placing two fingers on the glass, he noticed how much the sun that morning had warmed him.

He noticed some boys were playing near a fountain where a white marble elephant was standing over them.

- Now why don't you tell me what really happened? You want me to believe that you and the cardinal came a long way just for a glass of wine? –

- Look, I told you everything, believe me.

- Okay, since I'm sure you lied to me, you're coming with us now. Salvatore, we're taking the car for a ride.

The subordinate took the right keys between other bundles of keys, placed in a row on a wall board.

- Where are we going?

- You'll see him soon enough, ma'am. - answered De Simone.

Greta looked out the window looking for some landmarks, then noticed that they were heading towards Gianni's house, but said nothing.

- What? - Greta was shocked by what appeared before her eyes.

They stopped in front of the rusty entrance gate, the property from the outside seemed abandoned for quite a few years.

- You were here two days ago, right? Where did you come in from?

De Simone asked, intent on putting liquorice root in his mouth.

- Is there a back door or did someone open it?

- I... I came in through this driveway, and then a waiter greeted me at the door, but it wasn't like that here.

-What do you mean, it wasn't like that? Don't mock us, ma'am. We're here and she says she was here... but she wasn't here. Do you think you're going to continue?

- No, everything was new, clean, and when I went in the house, everyone was there, or almost everyone.

Greta hurriedly headed for the front door, squinting her eyes.

The two men followed her, she wanted to go inside.

She noticed that the windows were missing, the walls of the villa were full of cracks and covered with ivy and climbing plants. In the living room there was only a piano with broken keys and a large, ruined sofa.

Greta felt confused, thought someone was having fun behind her back, staging some kind of candid-camera show.

When the inspector asked her, once again, if that was the house where she had dined, she looked at the wooden table and the many chairs scattered around the room.

She noticed that many of them no longer had all four legs.

For a moment there was silence and you could hear the wind passing through the hole in the roof of the empty rooms where there were only rusty nets, without mattress.

- I swear to you, Inspector, that two days ago I was here, but the house was not in this condition. I had dinner with Gianni Serra and his wife Olga, there were waiters and guests, including Cardinal Tanzi. Gianni Serra I met him when he came to the office, he asked me to put a birth certificate in his file.

In agitation Greta was interrupted by De Simone, impatient.

- Madam, perhaps you missed a small detail. This is the Serra family's country estate, but it has never been renovated. I doubt that two days ago, it could be very different from what it is now. Now, we'll go to your office and get the certificate you mentioned earlier.


Still upset, Greta found herself searching the metal file cabinet of the legal department, looking for the file with Serra's papers, but did not find it.

Nor did she find anything among the files saved on the computer, nor among the appointments marked on the diaries.

It was all gone.

De Simone decided it was time to return to the police station to clarify other important points.

A policeman stopped the inspector as soon as he arrived at the police station.

- Inspector, you should come and see something. It's urgent.

They put Greta in a room, where she stayed for half an hour.

She tried to call Stella again but, receiving no answer, she left a message on her answering machine.

She was confused, she couldn't understand everything that had happened during that day.

About twenty minutes went by and the inspector appeared again, accompanied by a policewoman in uniform who stood next to her, while De Simone stood behind her desk, after taking off his jacket.

- Madam, I must inform you that your position has changed considerably in the last few minutes. You're under arrest for the murder of Cardinal Tanzi Barbuti. We'll be joined in a moment by the prosecutor, whom I alerted just now.

-What? -Are you kidding me? I didn't kill anyone, I swear! It's all a plot against me.

Greta got up quickly and in the excitement of the moment hit the chair that fell, making a dull noise.

The policewoman at her side placed a hand on her shoulder in an attempt to calm her, even more so to make her physical presence evident.

- Ma'am, we've just been handed a film that nails her to the murder.

Stop making up strange stories and start talking, telling the truth... I advise you to call a trusted lawyer immediately, if you don't do so, one will be assigned to you ex officio.

The tone of voice the inspector was speaking to you had changed considerably.

It was colder, more detached and professional.

He removed the liquorice root, now drained of its essence from his mouth, placed it in the ashtray on the desk and then nodded to the policewoman, with his index finger and a quick movement of his head, to take it to the room to the right of his office.

- I didn't kill anyone, I was there but I didn't do anything wrong.

The policewoman immediately interrupted her, making it clear to her that from then on, she would only be allowed to speak in the presence of a lawyer.

Greta asked for one of her own, unable to contact anyone.

They all seemed to have disappeared, from Stefano to Marco, moreover Stella didn't know where he was.

She was alone dealing with everything.

Shortly afterwards came a man in his fifties with glasses, with a classic leather bag who presented himself as the lawyer she had been assigned.

In the small, silent room there were Inspector De Simone, the prosecutor, the lawyer and a couple of other people unknown to Greta, who decided to tell everything from the beginning, just as he did with Stella.

- It's hard to believe your story, madam. –

The PM opened a box and took out the micro-camera that Greta immediately recognized.

- Well, I'm sure that will clear everything up. –

She exclaimed relieved.

The micro-camera was connected to a wall screen by strangers who, at that point, sensed they were technicians.

In silence, the images began to flow.

There was Greta, placing the bag just as she had indicated and, at the same time, in the background was very clear the outline of the cardinal snorting cocaine after having torn and rolled up the page of a Bible.

The woman, initially with her back to the camera, approached the bed and then sat astride the man's legs and tied his wrists to the headboard of the bed.

After a few seconds, the picture showed her grabbing a candlestick from a bedside table, of the large ones that are easily found in church, removing the large candle with her left hand.

You could clearly hear her voice say to him: "Now you mustn't move", tilt the candle towards the man's chest and let a few drops of wax drip down while His Excellency seemed very excited by the erotic game.

Greta was filmed as she turned towards the micro-camera looking at the lens with a disturbing stare.

Then, with a speed that contrasted the slowness of just before, place the candle on the bedside table, grab the candlestick and hurl the first slit at the priest's throat, the next two straight to the chest, one at the level of the liver and the last at the groin.

Everything took place in complete silence, it was no accident to cut his throat first, in the film it was clearly visible the stream of blood gushing from the inguinal artery and gradually staining the white sheet underneath, through an intermittent gush, which followed the residual heartbeat of the dying man.

The prosecutor asked to interrupt the vision, visibly shaken by such ferocity.

- Counsellor, I think it's clear to me the position of your client, no?

Greta was motionless in her chair, the whole time she watched the film as if she was watching a third-rate movie, those splatters her daughter liked so much.

She remained motionless with her eyes still glued to the off screen, trying to figure out where the film had come from, the policewoman invited her to follow her, raising her elbow.

- That wasn't me, that wasn't me, I was set up, do you understand? I don't recognize myself in that footage at all. God, what's going on?

She heard the men in the room talking to each other and systematically ignored it.

-What will happen now?

He asked Greta to his escort.

- the CPS fixes the hearing, the PM sets out the results of the investigation and the evidence justifying the arrest and possible remand for trial. The lawyer will explain it better in a little while, now you have to follow me.

He merely clarified in a calm but firm tone, then went out locking the door.

She sat and waited.

She heard voices outside the room.

She heard the sound of a key slip into the keyhole of the door and turn it open.

Her hands were sweating, she dried them on her knees. Greta got up from her chair and walked towards the man.

- Gianni? I need you to help me get out of here.

- No, you killed a man. You did it. There's proof.

- What are you talking about? You know how it is. You must help me. I must get out of here. I can't reach Stefano. You're the only one I have left. -

-No. This time you won't be able to lock yourself in a room to do whatever you want, not anymore.

I've decided it's time for you to leave for good. I'll tell you how it went.

You were in control, but I was still there.

Who do you think wrote that sentence in the garage? I saw what you did to that priest.

The moment you lost control for a second by dozing off, I took the camera I found in the garage and brought it here. You're just a part of her, that rotten girl is sick. You only live in her head and it's not real.

- What the fuck are you talking about? Now you're gonna tell me everything you know.

- Your name is Stella Couto Molinas. You were born in Cuba on August 11th. Your mother is Azuleya Couto Molinas and your father never recognized you.

When you were twelve, a neighbour of your grandmother's kidnapped you and kept you segregated and tied up in a cellar, raped you and then took turns with two of his brothers for a week.

And it was precisely to survive that trauma that your mind fragmented, fractured in four.

Over the years, three different satellite personalities have begun to take shape, acquiring depth and substance, giving themselves precise stories, slowly overturning Stella's original one.

The first to appear was the one you initially perceived as the imaginary friend, an adult named Stefano, like your father.

You reconstructed his personality based on the stories of your mother and grandmother, until you relived part of his story.

It was the most melancholic, the least structured of the three, full of guilt, the one that fully reflected the girl's mood.

Although he was the first personality to emerge, so relatively less complicated to make disappear, you had created him to perform the functions of loving father and consoler, able to calm your anxieties and reassure you in difficult times.

Marta was none other than your most creative, fragile, unstable and dependent alien personality, the transitional one.

It took us a while, several electroshock sessions, but in the end she gave in, succumbing.

- You tortured her. She was depressed and fragile. You were the shadows, the extent of her hallucinations... I should have known.

But she was destined to disappear anyway. I've taken the knife out of her hands a dozen times at least.

So you were the one who moved the ranks of us all. Eh good shrink! -

- Three years ago you came along, an angry, lying, exhibitionist revenge killer.

You came home bloodied, confessing what you had done, when you found out what a paedophile priest did in St. Joseph's Church in Rome.

For years there was only Greta, the one who was the longest fixated and developed, calcified in vengeance, in hatred and for this reason more difficult to eradicate.

Bringing Stella back to the surface was very difficult when they moved you here.

You know where we are, don't you? It's not a police station, it's a chamber in a psychiatric recovery facility. Look around you.

Greta crossed her legs and squeezed contemptuously into her shoulders.

- So what? I'm here. This is my reality and Stella's... a police station office, you're the alien.

- I brought you here, when everything got out of control, a directly proportional reflection of the lower stability of that scaffolding supported by the previous personalities, concreteness to unreality.

Greta began to stiffen. The mocking smile she had until a few seconds before printed on her face had vanished, aware of the trap.

- So you say that's unreal, me? Who gives you that certainty? We're both here, Stella and I. Look around. We're in a police station as far as I'm concerned. She's not here. I'm at the helm. The hub is in the galley. Now get out of here, don't ever come back.

- You're wrong. You can lock me out, but not her. Remember? Now you share the same landing, you accepted her help and therefore her presence.

She's here, to take back her life. –

Dr. De Meis asked the nurse to give Stella another dose of Migdalyn.

- I need her fighting now.

Stella found the courage to enter through the fourth door and found herself in front of the woman.

- Greta, it's all clear to me now. You're just my alter ego. As were Stefano and Marta.

- You want to play rough, little girl?

Okay, we'll play all the way, then. You think you can beat me? Useless little beast.

I'll lock you in the cellar. You remember the cellar, don't you? Do you remember who kept you alive then?

Who took matters into their own hands and agreed to get their hands dirty while you were overwhelmed with pain and ready to die because you'd given in?-

- No, you are nothing but a thought of mine, you don't exist except in my head, created and given birth by my imagination, the one I allowed to emerge in the moments when I felt fragile. Then you took over by relegating me to the deepest recesses of the ego. You limited me to that damn corridor, bringing out the other two.

Now thanks to the doctor I've found a way to bend, mortify your self-esteem, manipulate the false reality. Yeah, you underestimated my power of creation.

- And you think I don't get it? The little fat woman in the blue scrubs, the one who shoved the bucket out of the bathroom at the bar... The painting with the hospital on the wall. Gianni has always been the doctor, the occult director. –

- Yes, it's true. -De Meis intervened. -You sensed something. We just had to change our approach. The smell of hospital disinfectant used by an orderly in the room gave you a glimpse of where we really were.

- But you're wrong, Doctor, I am real. I am real because you made me real.

After a few seconds, Greta started talking to Stella again.

- Little girl, there were times when I heard you think the universe was just targeting you to hurt you. Poor little Stella... You'd rather be ignored, wouldn't you? But isn't it better to be dead than forgotten or worse, thought to be crazy?

At this point it seems that you have only two ways out: pretend that all this is real and disappear, or admit that it doesn't exist and go crazy spending your life in asylums.

It's your choice. Either way, I win. Take all the time you need to decide. I'm in no hurry.

I remind you that this is my reality and in this reality I'm the strongest... You haven't understood anything yet.-

- Maybe not, but I'm in a hurry. I have a life to live. Leave me alone, I won't let you corner me again, not anymore. I'm not afraid of your threats anymore. -

Stella's original identity began to show aggressiveness, just that rebellious reaction that De Meis had been waiting for a long time.

- Now you must do it, you must eliminate her. Face her as you did Stefano and Marta. Eliminate her, now! You have a letter opener on the desk to your right.

Stella then moved so much on the bed that she seemed to have a seizure.

- I can't do it. She's stronger than me.

- No Stella, that's not true. What's happening now? What's he doing?

- She disarmed me and she's hitting me, she keeps telling me I'm worthless without her. - She started crying.

- Adrenaline in the vein, Olga, now! - He ordered De Meis to the nurse.

- She mustn't give in now, not at this point, she might succumb and never re-emerge. -

Azuleya got up from the chair, brought her hand to her mouth, her breath had become wheezing.

- Stella, can you hear me? Fight it. You need to chase her away, you don't need her. -

In her illusory parallel reality, the girl was hit repeatedly but found the necessary shot to grab the letter opener and hit her in the heart.

Stella felt at that moment, in that mortal embrace, her release.

Although her body was immobile on the bed, the girl distinctly felt the fall that made her stomach jump.

A few small movements with her hand seemed to restore hope of success, and de Meis took the opportunity to give her directions.

- Stella, listen to my voice. Tell me where you are and what happened. -

- I hit her. I fell too, but I don't see her near me. I can't feel her anymore. -

- All right, now close your eyes, relax. Listen to my voice. You will be rescued and cared for.

When you wake up, you'll be calm and serene. At last you will realize you are alone, you will no longer hear voices or feel any presence foreign to your own. There will only be you. Now go to sleep. –

He kept tapping, with the precision of a metronome, the bic on the table.

The nurse gave her a sedative so that she could fix her words and the situation created on an unconscious level.

- Professor, tell me we did it. –

Azuleya, seeing her calm, breathed a sigh of relief.

- I don't know. I lost count of how many borderline situations we created to eliminate the Greta personality.

He put her glasses back on her nose, after cleaning them with a flap of her gown.

- We'll know tomorrow when I ask her about door number four. Otherwise we'll have to start all over again. -

Olga, attached the runoff to the cannula in her arm and connected an IV.

- This is to keep a venous access route open, to administer the drug if needed during the night. See you tomorrow, Mrs. Couto. Get some rest. –

De Meis politely greeted Azuleya and, for the first time, a slight veil of satisfaction settled on her face, caressing the girl's hand as she plunged into a deep sleep.

The next morning, Stella saw a man sitting on a chair get up and fill a glass halfway with water, then he brought the edge of the glass closer to her lips, helping her with his other hand to lift her head from the pillow.

-Welcome back, Stella. –

The man in a white coat told her.

- My name is Ottavio De Meis, I'm a doctor. Tell me, what's the last thing you remember? -

He clenched his forehead and shook his head.

- I know who you are, Doctor. I recognized your voice... The rest is all a blur. -

- Don't worry and try to stay calm, I'll explain everything. You're in a hospital and your mother is here with you, but don't get up suddenly, you might get dizzy, you might fall. –
Azuleya, who had been on the side-lines until then, came forward at the exact moment De Meis decided to leave the room and give the two women some time together.
She took her hands and gave her a kiss on the forehead.
-What happened, Mom? -
She asked by sitting on the edge of the bed. Then she put her hand to her forehead.
- I have a big headache. -
- I've missed you. Now get some rest. There's time to explain. –
Azuleya fixed her long raven hair, just as she did when she was a little girl.
The two braids, arranged with elastic bands recovered from the edges of a pair of latex gloves she found in a box, made her look younger than her twenty-three years.
The sedatives administered the day before and during the night continued to overwhelm the girl's physique, so much so that she couldn't help but lie down again and close her eyes, victim of an unnatural exhaustion.
- So helpless and at the same time so dangerous. You are the only thing I have, the most precious of all. –
Whispered Azuleya and sat back down.

# 4

## *OTTAVIO DE MEIS*

He graduated in medicine at the age of twenty-two and specialized in psychiatry at twenty-five.

He had chosen to take up the psychiatric profession not exempting himself from major risks: like all doctors, after all, he knew that psychiatry, unlike other specialties, would give a lot of satisfaction but just as much stress.

The exploration of the human mind, its functions and its intricate mechanisms, whether logical or illogical, had intrigued and fascinated him since high school.

The young doctor's life continued for the first ten years in the small private hospital of Borgo Sant'Eligia, not far from Rome, where he divided himself into four to visit the many patients who came from various parts of the region every day.

Since he was a boy they called him Ottavio " the bear ", because of his gruff and massive appearance.

The bright and dark eyes, hidden behind some glasses, from which he had memory, were in constant search. Slightly overweight, he was a big man, almost two metres tall, who easily intimidated his madmen, as he used to call them jokingly, so much to inhibit a priori any attempt of their reaction.

He had an advantage over many doctors.

Ever since his internship in the asylum, during his university years, he was the one who simply managed to immobilize and calm those who gave problems of discipline with a hug.

He never needed sedatives to calm someone, he used the tone of voice and particular words that at that moment intimately affected the patient, so as to establish an empathic bond.

He would do great things in psychiatry and it was clear to all his professors from the beginning. He used to wear his hand to his thick, reddish beard and wrinkle it when he was particularly intent on his study or his thoughts.

The experience gained over the years meant that the whole academic psychiatric field held him in the highest esteem, when he was still very young by university standards, he became a professor and obtained the position of director in the psychiatric unit of the University Hospital of Rome.

All at the expense of his private life: on the other hand, everything must have a price.

He had only sporadic adventures and no fixed woman to run away from or neglect for professional engagements, as happened disastrously in the past.

He was very attractive to women: there was nothing sexier than that big, fat man who appeared to have unassailable stability, able to control those impulses and anger that even as a young man could have got the better of him.

His silent self-confidence conveyed, without a trace of arrogance, the fact that he had nothing to prove to anyone.

What distilled it was a quiet sense of authority, an ability to read the movements of anyone's body and the rhythm of their breathing.

It possessed a sensual lingering over people that didn't necessarily have to do with looking them in the eye, but always required the desire to be vulnerable, and present at the moment.

A man with a sexual charge, able to control his impetus and with a firm grip on his ability to express himself.

The nurses were all crazy about him.

But for him, Stella had been his most important professional challenge for almost three years, and he still couldn't bring her back there, with him, in the present and in his presence.

Her fragile legs, her thin and melancholy face had impressed him from the first time he saw her.

She took him.

In all the ways a woman could take a man. He considered that "taking" a professional transport, not yet realizing how much that slim-legged girl had involved him deep down.

After several attempts at drug and psychological therapy, perhaps this time he had managed to take her out of the world she had created as a child.

He had studied for her, set up a research team with the proceeds of private donations, and developed a new drug, Migdalyn1235, with the help of a team. Five people were directed to her centre, including Stella.

The effect of the drug tested on laboratory guinea pigs was surprising.

And it also proved to be so in the very first human trials.

It acted on the amygdala, the emotional centre of the brain, triggering it like a sort of neuronal trigger.

By controlling the dosage and associating it with hormones, De Meis managed to achieve an unconscious physical and emotional reaction in his patients.

He discovered that this reaction could be triggered and piloted from the outside, isolating and selecting the various identities, through techniques of psychological conditioning or deep hypnosis.

It had happened to him several times, to trigger an emergency reaction in the subconscious of his patient's "A" personality.

He knew that stimulating the main parts of the brain responsible for the release of hormones, such as adrenaline and dopamine, would provide the ancestral reaction of combat or escape, in the personality present at the time.

The therapy with Stella worked thanks also to hypnosis, when Greta was induced to believe she was in a situation of immediate danger, conveying events in such a way as to bend her will, mortify her self-esteem, manipulate the fake reality.

He thought that the master's degree in mental manipulation achieved in the United States, despite what it had cost him, had given the hoped-for results.

For the first time, he felt proud of himself.

And it was also thanks to the technique he adopted that the castle made of so many little hearts of sugar inevitably collapsed, to make way for the dark ravine in which the real self, unable to face reality, had barricaded itself.

He had succeeded, with his neuroscientific research group, to "browse" the mnemonic systems to recall any useful information in the situation of fear.

His publications received a huge and unexpected critical success in the scientific community the following year.

So, even if that one girl didn't give the hoped-for results within the set time, in the end it turned out to be her greatest success.

The next morning would be a day that would mark the turning point in her career.

The proof that his method worked even on complex cases like Stella's, his protocols, would finally be recognized and applied in all cases of dissociative syndrome.

The right and deserved finale to a life dedicated entirely to study and experimentation.

- Stella, can you hear me? - He asked her to touch her with a finger right in the middle of her forehead, between her eyes.

With a lament she opened her eyes, signalling yes with her head.

- I need you to listen to me and do what I say. Relax, always focus on my voice. -

The doctor called a nurse to assist him.

He prepared a syringe and placed it in a steel tray, on top of the side table, of the swivel ones commonly used for meals in bed.

- Let's proceed with two cc's of Migdalyn in the vein. Take care, slowly.

After a minute, the time the drug was supposedly in her system, the doctor asked Stella if she could hear his voice.

- I hear it.

- Good. I want you to walk down the corridor, the bright white one, see it? I'm right by your side. We're gonna walk until you see some doors. Go past the first three, then stop in front of the fourth. -
- I've been here before, I'm cold. -
- I know dear, you were there yesterday. I'm with you, you're not alone.
Yesterday we saw the other three doors open, remember? Now you need to find door number four. The man's warm and reassuring tone of voice seemed to make her comfortable.
- Yes, I'm ahead of you. It's open and there's no one inside, just like the other three.
- That's great. You want to go all the way down the hall? If you look closely you'll see a ladder, I want you to go up to the top and get out of that house. You'll lock the door behind you, so that nothing and nobody can get out of there.
- I'm out. The front door of the building is closed. I turned and saw Greta banging on the window. But I can't hear her, I'm far away now.
- All right, now go to sleep.   Rest, it's all over.

# Medical Record No. 2985

The patient
Name: Stella Couto Molinas Age: 23 years old
Profession: none
Education: High school diploma Sent by: National Health Service

<u>Suitable for scientific experimentation
Migdalyn1235</u>

Main Diagnosis: Dissociative Identity disorder (multiple dissociative identity disorder)
Secondary: hyperkinesis.
In drug therapy and psychotherapeutic treatment three times a week at the local mental health centre.
Patient's history (based on the story made by family members and confirmed by the patient).
Born into a single parent family, the girl was brought up by her mother and grandmother with whom she lived together for fourteen years. before the crimes were committed.
Physical and intellectual development in the average until the age of twelve years.

The IQ detected is above average for age, school education, general culture and education received, have a clear and clear traditional imprint. Important is the ethnic-cultural context typical of the Cuban region where the girl comes from.

At the age of twelve she reported psychological trauma resulting from repeated sexual abuse conducted, as will be known later, by a 40-year-old fellow citizen of the family and his two brothers, individually and in groups.

The girl was held with coercion in the men's home for a week, until she was able to leave in a manner that was not ascertained or reported by the same.

She was found unconscious, in a marked state of dehydration (>10%) on her grandmother's doorstep.

Immediately was taken to the emergency room in the area, the little girl had physical, deep lacerations in the genital area compatible with the violence suffered, marked emo-concentration and reduced blood volume.

Initial renal and cardiovascular failure. Excoriations, circular lesions due to probable cigarette burns on one arm.

Cuts and ligament wounds.

Psychically all the typical signs of post-traumatic stress condition.

Delusional after-effects are probably due to this condition.

Her torturers were never found and convicted after a police report.

The family moved to Italy to a relative to remove the girl from the context in which the events and the violence took place.

This meant that the sexual abuse that occurred was neither discussed nor contested, although everyone was aware of the situation.

Total absence of figure, role and defensive actions by the father (male figure).

At the age of fourteen she was diagnosed as schizophrenic and began to build up her other personalities.

At the age of seventeen, she completes the "circle" as she calls it, formed by the other three personalities, two women and a man.

The predominant personality is that of a violent woman, Greta, who seems to have fed on the constant and unexpressed hatred resulting from past abuse.

She is arrested a few months later, still holding in her hands the candlestick used to commit the crime, the murder of a priest, such as Father Tanzi Barbuti in the sacristy of a church, catching him red-handed in the act of pedophilia. During the interrogation he presents himself as Greta. Subjected to a psychiatric evaluation confirmed the diagnosis of DDI.

This allowed her to face the trial, whose final sentence led to the declaration of not guilty for mental infirmity (the girl in fact was recognized as responsible for the facts, but not mentally present at the time of their commission) as a result of serious personality disorder, present at the time of the fact.

The girl was in a mental condition to exclude the ability to understand the meaning of the fact and to act in accordance with this assessment.

She arrived at our testing centre, on a voluntary basis, for the Migdalyn1235.

Upon arrival, the girl showed a marked impairment of the continuity of the sense of Self, accompanied by alterations in affection, behaviour, consciousness, memory, perception, cognition and sense-motor functions.

As per the attached report, she was confronted with all her personalities, thus allowing an initial albeit fragile fusion (integration).

But after a short time the personalities began to reappear, increasingly alienating the original identity.

So a change of approach was opted for, i.e. selection and disintegration.

The girl after about two and a half years of treatment responded excellently to the treatment.

Three sessions have been carried out since the patient stopped showing her multiple identities.

She was treated for sleep disorders for two more sessions.

The patient no longer mentioned her dissociative identity disorder in our sessions.
In addition, the acceptance of the trauma led to a change in therapeutic goals by accelerating the therapy procedures in the medium and long term.

The remission of the psychiatric pathology is therefore declared.

# 5

## *STELLA*

Stella closed the beauty case and put it on a chair. She thought that the zipper needed to be replaced, given the resistance to the closure.

She took her shoes out of the locker, sat down on the bed and tied them with the laces that a nurse had brought back just before.

She thought this was the first concession to her newfound sanity, if ever she had one.

-The doctor's waiting for you in his office to give you a copy of the chart and say hello. I wish you luck with everything, Stella. I'll miss you. If you ever need me, you'll know where to find us.

Olga hugged her and Stella smiled in recognition of the professor's assistant's Russian accent.

She walked down the corridor leading to the doctor's office, finding herself once again knocking on a closed door.

It was as if someone endowed with irony mixed with a hint of cynicism enjoyed making fun of her.

- Come in, Stella. So, how are you?

- Very good, Doctor. Thank you. And thank you for everything you've done for me. I'll never forget you.

- I did my job, but I won't deny you've been a tough guy. You control the ship again and whatever storm comes your way, the rudder is yours, don't ever forget it. This is a copy of the medical records. I had them photocopied before I left so I could give them to you without a formal request to the administration.
I've saved you a lot of time and bureaucracy. Your mother told me you want to go back to Cuba to your grandmother, is that true?
- Yes, it's true. I want to get back to my roots. My mother brought me here thinking she could find my father when I was sick, but she couldn't, so we have no reason to stay. –
- You've learned by being here that you can't fix everything but you can give everything a fix, you've faced your inner demons and in the sessions of the last few days. You have understood that you have to let go of sad and bad memories, so I won't tell you not to go to the same place that caused your illness, as your mother asked me to. -
- I knew it... Azuleya. She's trying so hard to keep me in Italy. -
-I trust you. -You know how to track me. –
De Meis reached out to greet her and shook her hand.
- Good luck.

- Thanks again. Thank you for trusting me, Doctor. When you want to take a holiday near us, don't hesitate to call us. Thanks again for everything. I'm running away now. Mom is downstairs in reception, she went to call a taxi.

It was a beautiful sunny morning in Rome, the air was fresh. After a long time, Stella no longer had a limited view of the structure's gardens, where access was allowed once a day, provided it didn't rain.

They were beautiful and well-kept, but the boundary wall delimited their boundaries.

A wall, the impassable limit of what was inside and what was outside, the mad inside and the "normal" outside.

As if there were only normal people outside and only madmen inside.

Stella was controlled by sight, a bit like all the guests of the structure, but this did not prevent, from time to time, to witness some brawl.

But the quarrels between them were never violent: it was neither war nor violence because there was no intention to harm the other, but to assert one's own reasons at all costs, most of the time making absurd and amusing assertions precisely because they were out of their minds.

Throughout her stay, she always sat on the same wooden bench, the one with one less board in the back, near the fountain with the elephant.

The lively gush of water coming out of the animal's mighty trunk on windy days broke along the edges of white marble with anthracite polka dots, a sign of the torment received from the many cigarette extinguishments of the madmen.

The roar of water reminded her of the wide waves with which the sea broke on the cliff.

Closing her eyes, she found her grandmother sitting at that very spot in the bay, looking at the ocean, while she had been waiting for years for her return.

She called her sea lily.

She, for Carmen, was just missing.

And just like all the scattered seeds of the sea lilies, she would return called by the waves of the swells, she would reach the dunes, protected by the goddess.

Just like that, as the seeds are protected, inside the very light cork that allows the buoyancy, as if they had a lifebuoy.

In her, that call was so strong, she felt she had to go home.

The taxi took the two women to her cousin Samuel who made himself available to host Azuleya, until Stella was ready to go home.

Samuel was married to Blanca and had two sons, twins who looked so much like him.

The apartment was in the suburbs, dignified and familiar, disorderly typical of people who work all day and have two small children at home.

Azuleya, during her daughter's months of hospitalization, managed to find work at the same cooperative where Blanca worked as a cleaner.

She had adapted in a sort of acquiescence, dictated by the need for money, so as to contribute to Samuel's household expenses and pay for the train ticket that took her to Stella's clinic.

They gave her the children's room, not having any other, spacious enough and with sky-blue painted walls.

That night Stella heard Blanca confide in her husband.

- They can't both stay here, they can find other accommodation. The children can't go on sleeping on the sofa bed in the living room.

- What do you want me to do? Put them on the street, kick them out? For God's sake. Blanca, they're family! After everything that girl's been through.

- Exactly! All the more reason to send her away.

- What are you really afraid of, Blanca?

- Do you know what she did or have you forgotten? She killed a man. I don't want her here in the house with the kids. I'm scared. I mean, what if she has a crisis?

She heard the man huffing.

- She's cured, she's on medication, you saw her at dinner. If she was dangerous, they wouldn't have let her go. - Blanca interrupted him.

- Yes, of course, because she'd be the first nut to go free, wouldn't she? If they don't leave in a few days, I'll leave with the kids. I'm warning you, Samuel!

- Shh! Keep your voice down, please! All right. I'll find a way to talk to my cousin. –
Stella closed her eyes.
The next morning she woke up her mother before the alarm and told her what she had heard.
- I'm sorry, Stella. Blanca's a bitch. -
- No, Mom, she's right. I would have thought the same thing, there are two children in the house and she's the mother.
It's in a mother's very nature to do anything to protect them. What do you say we go back to Cuba? -
- But why do you want to come back? Passing by the greengrocer's, on the corner near here I saw an apartment rental sign. With the money I have saved, we could make it. -
- Stay if you want, Mom. I'm the problem.
If I left, Samuel and Blanca would have no problem taking you in for a while and you could find a place without problems.
I've decided to go back to grandma's. Please, mama, let me go back to the bay. -
- There's no way I can change your mind, is there? –
Returning to the bay, seeing the places that were the scene of the violence, Azuleya was terrified of the possibility of a relapse.
Then she looked at her daughter and decided she had to do what was right and proper for her.

If she allowed her to carry her fears within her
all her life, Stella would remain an abused child
forever. Teach her not to be afraid anymore: this
was to be the ultimate goal of her mission as a
mother.
- Okay, fine. The money I saved up should be
enough for the trip. I want to see you happy now.
We'll go back to Grandma, that big rock head! -
The two women hugged and laughed like they
hadn't done in too long.
- I love you, Mom. –

The direct flight to Cuba No. 772, which left the airport on time, cost all Azuleya's savings.

The feeling of flying in a vacuum, of being leaning on clouds, of crossing entire nations in a few minutes, was priceless.

In contrast to her first flight, which she did not remember at all, Stella appreciated the beauty and grandeur of nature.

The mountains, rivers and cities, fields and oceans, unforgettable images and panoramas with the knowledge that she would never be able to visit them if not flying over them.

Floating in the air, gave her new feelings of pride, strength, security, excitement and happiness that accompanied her throughout the journey.

Although the next twelve hours would be a sort of space-time jump, Stella decided to ask her mother about Stefano.

- Can you tell me something? Did you really look for him, did you?

- Yes, I did. I rang the doorbell and his wife opened the door.

I told her I was a colleague of her husband's and that I'd like to see him again after a long time.

She lowered her head, hiding her disappointment and bitterness.

- He died when you were four years old, Stella, in a car accident.

- Okay, that's okay. That's the way it had to be. - Stella answered, turning her head towards the window.

De Meis' words came to mind when he told her about the effect of the train.

The little black hole in the soul, everyone has one.

There are those who waste time trying to fill it with selfishness and futility that do not belong to them and those who fill it with feelings, that emptiness cannot be filled in any other way, it is up to us to choose how.

The people at Martì airport, at the international arrivals, swarmed just like the industrious little ants that she had teased many times as a child playing with the ants.

She found the smells of her childhood and the many smiles that her people were accustomed to making, just like the beautiful wide one that Carmen reserved for her.

They arrived at the village at dinnertime and Stella went to bed early that night, right after taking her medicine.

Carmen walked nervously through the kitchen all night.

- I told you, but you never listened to me. She has to learn to control what she is. It won't be tablets that stop the spirits.

- Mom, please stop! She had a psychiatric disorder, do you understand? Enough with your stories of spirits and demons. Then you wonder why we left? Because of your medieval attitude, this is the 21st century. -
- You don't want to understand. Her father was with her when she was very young, she could see it!
- The psychiatrist said she'd developed the figure of her father as her imaginary friend.
- But she never saw him!
-Mom heard my stories, our talks, and she made a friend out of those memories, those descriptions.
- What about when she told you about the scar on her eye? She talked about it when she was four.
And we never talked about it.
I'm convinced that those women who took possession of her, too, were not personalities like the doctors say, but spirits! -
Azuleya, impatient, got up from the sofa and turned off the TV.
- Here we go again! As soon as you come back and insist on this nonsense. -
- Do you remember how she said she got out of the cellar alive?
A light entity released her and gave her two machetes. Then the column of water spinning from the earth to the ceiling.

Can you explain to me how a little girl did what she did to those three? She tore them to pieces and it was me who cleaned it all up. You think it was easy for me? There's not a night that I don't see that scene in my worst nightmares.

- She was sick, she was dying, it was normal she was delirious! She didn't tear anybody apart, nothing was ever found that would make you think about what she said. They left, those men ran away, and she went home with what little strength she had left. Adrenaline, Mom. You must have heard about the extraordinary reactions women and men have in stressful situations. And that's what happened to her. In Italy they treated her with the same hormones that allowed her to save herself when she was twelve. The machetes must have been found in the house. -

- I had a vision, going in there, of what happened, you and others can say what you want but I know what happened.

Carmen placed a wooden box tied with string on the table, then pulled out the machetes from the sharp blade and the blue handle, decorated with strips of leather and small shells.

- And these? These are Yemaya's sacred machetes. You know them well, even if you never accepted them.

I found them wrapped in a part of the sheet that wrapped you and you threw them back into the sea when Stefano left you.

They're the same... Why do you refuse to believe? She has the same powers as you and she has others whether you like it or not.

When I opened the door of the house and found her half dead on the threshold, she was holding them in her hand and her eyes were not normal but transparent, made of water. There was the fury of Yemaya's blood in her. And you know it!

- I don't know what I saw, Mom. But one thing is certain, I cannot accept these irrational speeches, these superstitions, my daughter's life depends on it. - Azuleya answered.

- You must, my daughter! You can't oppose a goddess. The moment you wished for your father on the beach, she gave you a daughter, too, and has been claiming her for a long time. Accept the fact that you're the daughter of the lady of the sea, and consequently your daughter will accept it too. –

She stopped for a moment, then continued.

- You never believed in divination and yet many times you had dreams that came true.

If you only experienced the gifts you have, you'd be amazed, and your daughter too. She has powers you can't even imagine, she used the machetes of justice that only the goddess can hold.

If she accepts her gifts she will be indomitable and cunning, her fury terrible, but she will also be sweet, brave and skilful hunter of evil in all its forms.

I believe she is the lady of the sea in physical form. Instruct her, that she may rule souls, as I did with you as a child. Then she'll be free to decide what to do and what to believe in, as I set you free. Otherwise they'll soon show up at her door again and there won't be any therapy for her.

Azuleya puffed, got up from the chair, put the steel blades back in the box, then tied it twice with string.

- That's enough, Mother! She's all right now. She felt nostalgic for the island and I brought her back.

The treatments keep her calm, and that's all that matters, but please swear to me we'll never speak of this again. And you will stay away from her with this talk. –

Carmen stopped talking to her daughter.

She thought it was pointless, she wouldn't listen to her.

That night she begged the goddess, begging her to give her time to make things right.

She still had in her head the scene that they found themselves in front of, in the house where she was held prisoner, during the police inspection.

On the west wall of the room, the iron beam that propped up two walls and to which she still had attached ropes wrapped in an inextricable tangle, surely used to tie the child.

Below it, a filthy mattress thrown on the floor, a small bottle of water, a loaf of bread and all around the signs of an obligatory stay. The police could only ascertain what had happened. They took it for granted that the hole, about thirty centimetres wide, was the result of the subsidence of the ground following Hurricane Moses the previous year.

- They fled when they realized the little girl had escaped. I don't think they'll see the rogues again.

But Carmen in her heart, she knew that things hadn't gone that way, she could see the signs of Yemaya's fury. On the ceiling there were circular signs that confirmed Stella's version, the one complete with details that the police never knew. She told of how the earth opened up, a column of water came up to the ceiling and a woman gave her machetes with which she tore the stunned men to pieces.

Then the water retreated from where it had come from, taking with it what was left of the three. Not a drop of blood in that room, on the contrary Stella, although she had no cuts, was covered with them.

Azuleya went into the room, hid the box in the back of the closet, so that her mother had no access to it to show it to Stella.

Carmen, who had experienced hardships and
trials in life that made her the strong and
determined woman she was, thought for the first
time that perhaps the secret to a happy old age
was a pact with loneliness.

That night she moved between the sheets,
feeling the lucidity of the moon, wondering
what would have happened to her daughter and
grandaughter if she had not been there at dawn.
She sensed that at dawn, if she was not there,
everything would have to be readjusted in a new
perspective. She opened the balcony, dragged
out the wooden chair in her room and looked at
the bay under the strange light of the moon.

Familiar though it was, the view seemed to her a
new spectacle. She knew the village inch by inch,
every roof, every window, every noise and even
one by one all its inhabitants.

It was a place where disorder was only
appearance.    She looked for the packet of
cigarillos leaning a little farther on the flowerpot
a few hours before, then she started smoking by
leaning her arms against the railing.

She hadn't liked smoking for a long time, her dry
throat and coughing reminded her of how much
she had abused it in the past, but the thin smoke
she drew figures when it came out of her mouth
reminded her of who she was and the
temporariness of everything.

Carmen, she still had the charm of yesteryear. She had broken several hearts among the men of the village, with her amber-colored skin, which emphasized and highlighted her big eyes, black and proud.

Under the last onslaught of the night, she remained in that position for a good piece of silence tasting, then decided that in the morning she would walk around with her usual smile, despite the atrocious heat wave on the island and despite the premonitions she had about her granddaughter.

She felt that something was changing, the sea had never lied to her.

At dawn she went down to the beach, saw that the rough sea at night had left a blanket of *aguamalas* on the shore, small blue jellyfish with a swollen crest and a long purple tail.

A few days later, putting clean sheets in her mother's room, Stella felt a strange attraction towards the closet.

It was as if something told her to open it, a temptation she could not resist.

She looked inside and saw nothing in particular. Then a space between her clothes.

The thin planks, now spaced out at certain points on the back board, gave her a glimpse of something underneath.

The wooden box had the four corners decorated with ciprias, while in the centre, finely carved, a snake with a moonstone in place of the eye.

She removed the string and opened the box, then lifted the bundle that was kept inside.

She moved the cloth inside which something was wrapped, until she saw the sacred blades.

She saw the two crossed snakes on the handles of which he had lost his memory and found the feeling of power to the touch.

- Hey, beautiful, where have you been? –

In her eyes, dull and foggy with medicine, the leap of life seemed to revive them, a new light pervaded them and within himself he felt the strength and energy of the sea making its way.

She remembered everything.

She felt powerful again, like that night when he killed his jailers, a moment after she begged her to let them go.

She remembered two big, big men, falling one after the other, under the blind fury of a skinny 12-year-old girl, and a third running away.

She remembered how she found by chance, the blades under the mattress and the precise sensation when she felt them sink easily into the flesh and the desire to do so, the inhuman screams and the hurricane that swept everything away.

She understood that this power, of whatever nature and origin it was, would manifest itself again, when she would lose all hope and invoke the end.

When a moment before she exploded with anger, her hand would arm itself again...

# ABOUT THE AUTHOR

Maria Tenace was born in 1975 in San Marco in Lamis, in the province of Foggia, but is currently living in Guidonia Montecelio in the province of Rome, with her partner and a twelve-year-old daughter.

After graduating from classical high school, she moved to Rome to attend a degree course in Biological Sciences at the University "La Sapienza".

Always passionate about symbolism, history of popular traditions and a lover of reading, especially noir books and thrillers, she tries her hand at writing.

In 2017, she participated in a literary contest in the non-fiction section with her work "Symbolicum: the main myths of creation", arriving among the finalists of the national competition for debutant writers "ilmiolibro".

With "The Fourth Door", her first novel, she experiments with the writing of a psychological thriller, a synthesis of his interests in history and science.

www.ingramcontent.com/pod-product-compliance
Lightning Source LLC
LaVergne TN
LVHW020335200726
843507LV00012B/2373